This is a work of fiction. Names, characters, businesses, places, events, and incidents are either the creations of the author's imagination or real websites or products used in a fictional manner. Any resemblance to actual persons, living or dead, or actual events is purely coincidental.

Author's Acknowledgement:

I'd like to thank John Lordan of the LordanArts YouTube channel for his kind guidance and insight into the world of YouTubers, websleuths, and the dramatic cases of missing persons and unsolved murders. John spends a great deal of time interviewing the families of victims, being their ear and their voice.

Thank you, John, for being the Story Consultant on this work of fiction, and for fighting the good fight.

For Gary.

Doug!

Nice to see you again! Enjoy something a little different!

Frederick H. Crook

Wraithworks

Frederick H. Crook

Chapter One

*G*ary Wraithworth looked into the depths of the camera lens and powered through the sad news. Another missing person had been discovered in the worst condition imaginable. She had been sexually assaulted, killed, and mutilated after the fact. As he always did, he took solace from the fact that his wife, Tera, stood behind the camera, watching him with her kind, pale blue eyes. Try as he might to prevent it, Gary's eyes glistened as he spoke.

"So, there we have it, everyone." He halted to clear his throat and his eyes shifted left to right and back to the lens again. "My condolences go out to this young woman's parents. I can only begin to imagine what they're going through right now. Our thoughts and prayers are with them."

He summed up the case and then went through his sign-off, letting the audience know they would see him in the next video, scheduled for upload the next day.

Tera cut off the camera and set it on the desk in front of him. As she usually did at the end of such a hard recording session, she stepped to him and kissed him on the forehead.

"You okay?" she asked.

Gary nodded and sighed heavily, saying nothing.

"I'm going to put something together for dinner. Are you going to start editing now?"

"Yeah, I'd better get on it," he answered and moved his laptop from the credenza behind him to its place on the desk. "We have to be at the airport by eleven tomorrow."

"Okay," Tera said and quietly left, closing the den's door behind her.

Gary opened his video editing software, plugged the camera into the computer, and began to edit the piece. The sadness he felt for the dead girl was heavy, and he knew from experience that it would take some time to get over it.

He paused for dinner and an hour of television with Tera, and by ten that night, he was back to editing. With the process well-practiced, he was able to finish the video, make a backup, and turn in just after midnight.

The couple awoke the next morning and made the cab ride to Minneapolis–St. Paul International Airport.

Gary Wraithworth enjoyed his minor celebrity status. Just by wearing a hat or putting on sunglasses, he could walk through a store, an airport, and even some trade shows without being recognized.

As he walked through the airport with Tera, no one gave them a second look. This would change when they arrived at the convention, as the hall would be crawling with people that had seen and subscribed to his YouTube channel.

The flight to Denver was uneventful, which was just how Wraithworth liked it. He was no fan of flying, but his schedule and that of Tera's job at the accounting firm did not allow them time for a road trip.

TruCrimeCon was only in its second year in the Colorado Convention Center. They attended last year, so they knew where to find the event staff room to check in.

A young female volunteer issued Gary and Tera their ID badges and escorted them through a maze of tables, curtained-off sections, and vendor sites to his table. This was where they would spend the weekend meeting fans, signing autographs, and selling t-shirts and hats. A large sign hung from the wall of curtains behind their chairs. *Wraithworks* was printed in a red, fanciful font against a black background that featured yellow police crime scene tape. An enlarged photograph of Gary was set below the moniker.

"Who's that smug asshole?" Gary jokingly asked Tera in a lowered voice.

"Such a big head," she answered and giggled. "Must be some movie stah."

It was a long-running joke between them. Wraithworth had spent the years of his youth trying to break into acting. He had starred in a few commercials and met Tera on the set of one. Three years of dating and seven years of marriage later, both were in their early thirties and happy.

The box of t-shirts, baseball caps, buttons, and stickers they had shipped ahead had been placed under the table. Tera dragged it out and opened it. Gary helped her arrange the paraphernalia along the white tablecloth.

They both settled into light conversation as other YouTubers, social media stars, and even a few authors arrived.

Gary took a deep breath and let his mind wander to his next video project to settle the butterflies in his stomach. The show was minutes from opening.

***

The people flooded into the convention hall as soon as they were granted entry. Small squads made a beeline for their favorite personalities, and Gary Wraithworth had gathered his share. Soon he was answering questions about cases, posing for selfies, signing autographs, shaking hands, and selling merchandise.

The hall thrummed with the voices of thousands of attendees for hours. For Gary and Tera, it did not seem like such a long day. The fans of *Wraithworks* were enthusiastic and supportive, and the naysayers were minimal.

Time flew by and, at five o'clock, the event ended for the day. As Gary and Tera packed the t-shirts and caps into the boxes and stowed them under the table for the night, a tall man in a black overcoat strode up to them, smiling.

"Mr. Wraithworth," the mocha-skinned and stout stranger greeted with his hand reached forward.

"Hi there," Gary replied as he shook it, trying to sound jovial. There were always stragglers at these events and all he wanted at the moment was a cheeseburger, a beer or three, and a quiet evening in their hotel room upstairs.

"Nice to meet you," the enthusiastic young man chirped. His grin displayed well-cared-for teeth. "I'm David Greely. I don't suppose you've ever seen my channel. It's *Greely's Reels.* That's reels with a 'z.'"

"Uhh…you know, it sounds familiar," Gary answered routinely. He never wished to hurt anyone's feelings, but there were countless

YouTubers with their own channels and he found out long ago that he could not keep track of them all.

"It's cool if you haven't," David conceded. "I'm not offended at all. I have less than half the number of subscribers you do."

Wraithworth gave a short chuckle and a shrug in response. The steady gaze from his wife told him she wanted to leave. Dinner was calling to her, too.

"Anyway, I hoped to run into you here," David said and reached into his overcoat's inner pocket. He offered Gary a thumb drive. "I was going to mail it to you, or maybe email a link to a video sharing site but delivering it in person is way more secure."

Gary refrained from taking the item from Greely's hand. "And what's this?"

"Oh, just a couple of videos I'd like you to see," Greely said and raised his other palm in a gesture of innocence. "These are lower resolution for file space. I'd be interested in your opinion."

Gary followed his wife's lead and began to step in the direction of the side exit. "What kind of video is it?"

David looked around him before answering in a quieter voice. "Some dashcam crime scenes."

"David, there's no shortage of those on the 'net," Gary said and picked up his pace.

"Mr. Wraithworth, please," Greely pressed, keeping up with the couple. "I promise you, you're going to want to see this."

Tera reached the door and opened it, holding it for her husband. Her expression had gone blank. Gary knew this was a hint to shut this fan down and quickly.

"Look, David," Wraithworth said once he had gone through the door, "I get a lot of people sending me things. Why don't you email it to the address on my site? My producer can look at it."

"Mr. Wraithworth, I think it would be better if you just had a look."

Tera stopped and turned on their visitor, stepping partway in between the two men. "Look, buddy. He told you what to do with it, now if you don't mind−"

"Please," David said calmly. "I'm not trying to be rude, honest. Please just have a look at the videos. There are only four and they're short. And by the way, Mrs. Wraithworth, I know you're his producer, so why don't you take it?" He held out the thumb drive to Tera, his eyebrows pinned high on his forehead, his winning smile unfaltered.

Tera sighed and took the thumb drive. "Fine. We'll have a look."

Greely pressed his palms together as if to pray and gave several short bows. "Thank you so much."

Gary stuck out his hand to give David's a shake. It was usually a good tactic for ending a conversation. "It's great meeting you. We'll take a look and get back to you. Okay?"

"You bet, Mr. Wraithworth," David said as he vigorously shook Gary's hand. "I appreciate you both. My booth is on your row, east of you. Third from the end. Or email me." David let Gary's hand free and began to walk backward, toward the door they had just walked through.

"Okay, David," Gary agreed and waved, allowing his wife to tug him away by the arm.

***

Gary and Tera spoke of the encounter over dinner at the brew pub across the road. Tera was irritated over the incident, but Gary reminded her that Greely seemed kind enough and was far from their worst encounter. After a while, and a beer apiece, their humor resurfaced, and conversation turned to other topics.

Later, in their hotel room, Gary and Tera relaxed, intent on getting their rest for the next day of the convention, which would have them both occupied for two hours longer.

Tera stepped into the shower while Gary scanned through channels on the television on the wall opposite the king-sized bed. He opened his laptop and went through his email and social media accounts. The fan interaction was far livelier during conventions, but Gary answered much of the first salvo of messages.

He was about to close his laptop for the night when he remembered David Greely and his thumb drive. He set the computer aside and left the bed in search of Tera's purse, finding it on the counter next to the sink in the hall. He never felt comfortable fishing through his wife's things, but he remembered seeing her slip the small drive into the side pocket.

His fingers found the item and he withdrew it. He eyed the storage device as he walked back to the bed and muted the television. Instead of plugging the drive into his laptop he launched his browser and clicked on the shortcut to YouTube. In the search, he typed '*Greely's Reelz.*' A list of videos appeared; the top one featuring a smiling David Greely wearing the same black overcoat. It had been posted that day and was a short piece recorded in front of his booth in the convention hall.

Wraithworth played the video but there was no mention of himself, only a greeting to fans of the *Greely's Reelz* channel and his expression of his gratitude for them. David seemed a perky, perhaps a bit over-excited individual, but that was not unusual for a YouTuber. Gary navigated to David's channel and scrolled through the list of videos. There was the usual mixture of ghost investigations, conspiracy theories, a few urban explorations of abandoned buildings, and reviews of movies and books.

From the persona, and the collections of apparently well-meaning videos, Gary disregarded the thought that the young man would have implanted anything malevolent in the memory device. He shrugged and plugged it into his computer just as Tera turned off the water in the bathroom.

The folder popped up on the screen displaying five files, the first four were videos and the fifth a text file. He opened the first one and it played in a small window.

What appeared to be a security camera was focused on the sidewalk in front of a hotel. It was nighttime, and it was raining. The scene was well-lit by street lights as well as the glow from the lobby windows. Gary judged the height of the camera to be some fifteen to twenty feet above the sidewalk. He presumed it was mounted to the corner of the building, giving him a wide shot of the area beneath the hotel's canopy and part of the street.

After a few seconds, a black limousine came into the right of the frame, stopping at the curb and lining up the doors with the canopy. The driver jumped out and went to the other side of the car, and then opened the door for his passenger.

Exiting the car was an older gentleman, as could be seen from his white hair. He made his way to the front of the hotel as the driver walked toward the trunk, out of sight under the canopy.

As the older man approached the door, a third man entered the scene, moving quickly. He was taller and of a similar hair color. The limo's passenger backed away from the newcomer, who strode straight at him. It looked like the man had a gun in his right hand.

The older man moved out of the camera's view and the stranger followed. The driver reentered the picture, running in the direction the other two went. He was reaching into his suit jacket for a pistol, Gary assumed, but never got a chance to draw it. In a cloudy blur, the driver dropped to the sidewalk. There he remained motionless.

"Holy shit," Gary murmured.

The video cut to the aspect of a police car's dashcam. The date was displayed in the lower right-hand corner. It was March of 2017 and, like the first part of the video, it was a rainy night, leading Wraithworth to assume it was part of the same incident. There was still no sound.

The police cruiser was in pursuit of a dark gray car, speeding crazily along the wet pavement. The cruiser's red and blue lights reflected and flickered against street signs and puddles.

The gray car sped through a red light, almost leaving the ground when it struck a dip in the road. The officer braked hard as he checked for traffic then continued through.

Tera came out of the bathroom wearing a hotel robe and a coiled towel on her head. "What's that?" she asked.

"Greely's vids," Gary answered distractedly.

"Oh." She sat on the bed and stared at the silent television.

Without taking his eyes from the laptop screen, Gary said, "You can put the volume up if you want. There's no sound on these."

Tera took the remote and unmuted the television. After a moment, she changed the channel to a familiar sitcom that Gary could ignore as he continued watching the drama on his laptop.

The gray car had taken a number of fast turns and the police officer expertly followed. Together they left the center of whatever town was in the video and the scene became a high-speed chase through a residential neighborhood. Here, the cruiser came close enough that it tapped the right rear quarter of the gray sedan. It spun out, struck a parked car, and stopped. It was a perfectly executed Pursuit Intervention Technique, or PIT maneuver as it was commonly called.

The police cruiser came to a hard stop and the officer lit up the disabled car with his headlights and spot. Two more cruisers arrived, and more flashing blue and red lights flooded the scene.

Three officers approached the vehicle with guns drawn. The gray car had tinted windows, so it was impossible to see inside. Bravely, one officer reached the driver's door and tried the handle. The door was locked. The officer pulled out his tactical baton and shattered it on the third impact.

The door was opened, but Gary could see the officers struggling to find anyone inside. The video ended a moment later with the three policemen scanning the area with their flashlights.

Curious, Gary opened the text file and saw that it was written to explain each video. Reading the paragraph introduced as 'Video 1', he let out a low whistle.

"What?" Tera asked. She had propped herself on pillows and begun to fall asleep.

"I don't know about this," Gary answered, "but the description of this first video says it's the assassination of Thomas Mackelby, the mayor of Bloomsburg, Pennsylvania. He was the one that was running for state rep or something."

As Gary's producer, Tera knew his list of investigative videos well, even the cases they had decided not to do. "Wait, did you say Mackelby? There wasn't enough coverage to look at that murder."

"I know."

"But you're saying there's video of it."

Wraithworth had already opened a search engine for the story and, having backed the video to the beginning, verified the name of the hotel, which was on the canopy. He turned the laptop so Tera could see it.

"Look, the hotel's right. The Van der Veer in Bloomsburg." He forwarded the video to the pursuit. "The date Mackelby was killed is the same in this police vid. March the nineteenth."

"Shit," Tera whispered. "Where did he get this? I've never seen this."

"I don't know. I haven't either."

Gary let her watch it and then clicked on the next video. A hotel hallway appeared. The carpet was maroon with flower pattern, bracketed by white walls interrupted by doors made of dark wood.

Standing in the range of the security camera was a tall blonde teenager, talking with a tall man with short gray hair. The girl, dressed in jeans and a t-shirt, did not appear to be happy. She looked about nervously, perhaps for an opportunity to escape. The man, a whole head taller than she, kept her uncomfortably close.

"Holy shit," Tera blurted.

"What?"

"That's...um−" she tried to explain, pointing to the monitor with one hand and snapping the digits of the other.

"The girl? Yes, she does look familiar," Gary admitted. He had featured so many missing girls on his YouTube channel that their names and faces became hard to retain.

Without a hint of what was coming, the gray-haired man's right arm raised as the blonde glanced away. He struck out with a large fist, connecting with her left cheek. She dropped to the carpeted floor as if the life was knocked from her.

"Shit!" Gary shouted as Tera gasped.

The man turned, showing a white shirt and tie as he leaned down, hoisted her up onto his shoulder, and strode down the hallway, away from the camera.

"That bastard," Tera growled.

They were transfixed on the little laptop screen. The video continued from another camera, this one outside the hotel and focused upon the parking lot with a dark blue, full-sized SUV parked at the curb.

"What's going on here?" Tera asked in an expectant whisper.

As if in answer, the gray-haired man appeared with the unconscious blonde draped over that same shoulder. He approached the truck, opened the rear door, and chucked her inside. Her captor slammed the door and strode to the driver's side. The SUV drove off the screen a second later.

"Look at that guy over there," Gary pointed out and backed up the video. A bystander, on his way to his car on the far right of the screen, watched the whole scene. Some twenty seconds after the vehicle left, the bystander's light-colored sedan pulled out of the space and went the other way.

"There's nothing he can do," Tera said. "Besides, the captor looks like a cop."

"Or FBI," Gary commented as he switched to the text document. He read, but Tera read faster.

"Mishka Bellacosta? We did a show on her," she exuded. "Last summer, I think."

"Yes," he replied and nodded excitedly. "She was last seen in Dallas. I've never seen this recording either."

"They never found her, right? Gary, what the hell is going on? Where...how did this Greely guy get this stuff?"

"You're right, Mishka's still missing. I don't know what's going on."

The description of the second video indicated that the gray-haired individual was the same man that drew the pistol in the first video, presumably shooting and killing Thomas Mackelby to death.

Gary brought up the first video, leaving the second one open. He paused the Mackelby video at the point where the assailant entered the frame and compared it with the man in the second.

"I'll be damned," Wraithworth whispered.

"Perhaps, but not today," came Tera's practiced response. It was another running joke. "That *is* the same guy."

"Looks like it," Gary agreed.

Gary read the descriptions of the next two videos aloud. "The gray-haired tough guy is seen here taking part in the abduction of Bill Welks."

"No! The novelist?"

"Apparently." He continued reading. "'He is seen here on a New Orleans police car's dashcam getting out of a Louisiana State Police cruiser and taking Welks into custody for public intoxication.'"

"Impersonating a cop?"

"He would have to be," Gary answered. "Mishka went missing in Dallas. Mackelby was killed in Pennsylvania."

"This dude gets around," Tera said.

Gary initiated the third video and it was as described. The gray-haired man was featured prominently, wearing a state trooper's uniform and conversing with New Orleans police officers for a time before stuffing Welks in the back of the State cruiser and driving off. Bill Welks was still missing.

The last video was of the same man in the act of holding up a convenience store in Atlanta, Georgia. He wore sunglasses, but by now, Gary had become accustomed to the man's physical attributes. The squared shoulders, short-cropped hair, and long arm reach, gave him away.

Just as the Wraithworths were wondering why the man had chosen to knock off a store, Gray Hair turned his pistol on a customer and pulled the trigger three times, dropping the man to the tile floor. With that, the shooter quickly departed. The victim was an attorney, David Greely's text described, by the name of Martin Schofield. At the time, Schofield was the head of a firm that was bringing a lawsuit against the oil companies responsible for spills in the Dakotas and Texas.

"Wow," was all Gary could say once the last video was finished. He closed his laptop and removed the thumb drive.

"It is one messed up planet out there," Tera decided.

"So it would seem," her husband responded.

"What do we do now?"

"What *can* we do?"

"I think we need to interview Greely," she suggested.

"As in, an interview for the channel?"

"Not yet. I mean talk to him tomorrow at the show. Or afterward at dinner. Something."

"Great idea," Gary said. "I'll find him tomorrow."

The couple turned in for the night, but Gary had a hard time relaxing. The bed was a little too soft, but mostly, his mind kept him awake as his memory played the details of the videos over and over, generating a great amount of questions.

<u>Chapter Two</u>

*T*he dream was like so many others. It was of a girl he had featured on a show so many years before. She was the same age as when she had gone missing. Some part of him always told him that what he was seeing was impossible. Nevertheless, he routinely responded by walking after the child and trying to communicate with her.

The circumstances differed from dream to dream. The setting was never the same, and his abilities or disabilities changed. That night, he could not speak, though he could fly.

The child had light brown hair and wore a parochial school uniform. She was scared and ran impossibly fast.

He willed his body to keep up and left the ground with arms outstretched. He needed to track her, rescue her, and get her home. Gary knew no other purpose in this or any nightmare in which she appeared.

He flew like a superhero, chasing the lost girl down streets set between unlit skyscrapers, vacant of pedestrians and clear of vehicles. Try as he might to call out, no sound left his mouth, though she cried out in fright continuously. He wanted to tell her that her parents missed her and that he wanted only to get her home, but his message could not be heard. After following for many blocks, he found that he was not gaining on the girl.

He wished his body to fly faster, snapping his palms to his sides. At first, it worked, and he closed on the supernaturally fast child. She looked over her shoulder, saw him, and hung a left turn at the next intersection. Gary followed, only to find his body assailed by a great wind. Dust was hurled into his eyes. After a moment of no forward momentum, he was exhausted and dropped to the pavement. He lay there with his limbs sprawled out and his eyes closed.

Next came rain and thunder.

He lifted his head in time to see the girl disappear into the misty gloom.

***

Gary opened his eyes to the morning sunlight breaking through the parting of the drab green curtains. He squinted to read the time on the clock. There was more than an hour left of sleep before they had to rise and prepare for the day, but the girl in his dream would refuse to let him go. She would be there if he returned.

Gary lay in the strange bed for some time before he quietly left it. He sat in the chair in front of the small desk, where he had left his laptop. He inserted Greely's thumb drive and began to watch the videos once more.

His mind tried to reconcile the reason for the same man to be involved in these murders and abductions. He wondered what connected the victims.

Mishka Bellacosta was a runaway that had gone missing from her Dallas home nearly two years ago. She was a stripper and possibly a sex worker, but it was never proven. She would be twenty-three years of age if she was alive.

As for the author, Bill Welks, Gary had never featured the man on his channel, but he found by looking up the name on a popular book seller's site, that he should have. Welks wrote many fictional novels of political intrigue, some thrillers, and two nonfiction books on corporate fraud. It was plausible that Welks had been killed for something he had written.

Gary shook his head clear. He realized there was not enough information given in the text file and he was not yet awake enough to think anything through. He thought about sending an email to Greely but decided against it. He would catch up to him at the convention when he had a free moment to walk to Greely's booth.

Sometime later, the clock alarm sounded, jolting him from his dozing in the semi-comfortable chair and stirring Tera, well-covered under the sheets.

***

Still yawning, Gary walked behind Tera as they made their way to the booth. He nodded and mumbled morning greetings to those that initiated communication. At the table, he set his coffee next to hers and helped her place their items on the table. All the while, he kept an eye out for David Greely.

Once everything was placed, the couple sat and were quiet as they drank their coffee. Gary grabbed his *Wraithworks* cap and snugged it down, keeping the ceiling lights from his eyes. Tera would put her cap on once she saw the fans begin to wander in.

"Hey," Tera said and nudged him with her elbow.

"Huh," he replied flatly.

"You okay?"

"Yeah. I just have Greely's vids on my mind."

"I don't doubt it," Tera took up. "I've been looking for him."

"You too, huh?"

Tera smiled. "I can't see down the aisle. If you want to take a walk that way, go ahead. We have about twenty minutes."

Gary agreed. Other attendees were either getting ready or were set up and chatting with their table-neighbors. He waved to those he knew, said his good mornings and then heard his name being shouted.

"Hi!" he called once he turned to the voice. He had almost missed one of his favorite fellow YouTubers, Daisy Hersh. The young redhead's table had been blocked from view by a small crowd of fellow YouTubers and she had almost missed Gary stroll by.

"Hey, Gary!" she shouted and came around front, past all the eyes rudely ogling her. She rushed up and hugged Wraithworth high on the neck.

"Oh!" Gary laughed. "Careful, you'll get me in trouble with the wife."

Daisy let him go and laughed. "So, how've you two been?"

"Oh, very good. The channel's reached a hundred thousand subs, finally."

"I noticed! That's wonderful," she said in her usual bubbly manner. "You deserve it. You guys do great work."

"Thanks," he replied and blushed.

"So, where were you headed?"

"Oh, I was just looking for David Greely. Do you know him?"

"I sure do," she answered in a quieter voice. "He told me that he would be contacting you here," she added and held his gaze.

"Yeah," Gary said and nodded. "I'm going to talk to him about what he gave me."

"Do that," she encouraged and stepped back. "I've told him I'm in."

"Really? Good to know," Gary said, though he was unclear about her meaning. "Talk later?"

"You bet!"

Gary walked on and, as he approached the end of the row, he found Greely sitting at his table with his feet, adorned with high-top sneakers, crossed upon the table. The YouTuber was reading a thick paperback.

His table offered pamphlets and cards about his channel and a *Greely's Reelz* t-shirt was placed on a mannequin torso at his left. A caricature of Greely took up the middle of the shirt, exaggerating his physical features. Clutched in Greely's cartoon hands were a pair of film reels.

"Good morning," Gary called as he approached the table.

David's head lifted abruptly and, upon seeing who it was, his smile beamed. "Good morning, Mr. Wraithworth," he said and struck out his hand as he stood. The two men shook. "I take it you've had a look at—" He stopped speaking as his dark eyes darted around, checking to see if others were close enough to overhear. "—my files. I'd be interested to hear your thoughts."

"Well, if they're accurate, it would make quite a story."

"And you're wondering why it isn't already," David presumed.

"To say the least. Where in the world did you get all of that?"

"There's more," Greely said, and his smile changed from being jovial to conspiratorial. "Much more. All featuring that agent with the gray hair."

"Agent?" Gary found himself whispering.

David matched Wraithworth's volume. The conversations of the other attendees surrounded them. "It's been uncovered that he's FBI, but just think of the videos on that drive. And think about the abduction of Bill Welks. You have to ask yourself how he got that Louisiana State Police uniform *and* cruiser."

"I was wondering about that."

"A former trooper says that car was listed as being in the service bay that day. All day."

"And no one has copies of that vid? Is no one looking into that? How is that possible?" Gary gave a curt shrug.

"My source is with the New Orleans police and was paid to destroy it."

"But he kept a copy?" Wraithworth pressed in a whisper.

David nodded and stepped around his table to join Gary in the aisle.

"Okay." Gary checked the time on his cellphone. "They'll open in a few minutes. What are you planning? A vlog on your channel?"

David chuckled and raised his hands, showing Gary his palms. "No, man. Not on *Reelz*."

"Well, then what?"

"I was thinking of creating an alternate channel…another persona, another name."

"Ah, and then have other YouTubers share it," Gary presumed as he stroked his chin beard.

"Exactly," Greely said. "I can go to a different hot spot everyday if I want, so my IP address stays hidden."

"And you showed me these so I cover the story?"

David beamed. "I was certainly hoping for a little support from a star of your caliber." His eyebrows shot up. "There are others, too.

We're hoping these go viral while protecting the people involved in uncovering the footage and writing the report."

Gary said nothing for a moment as he contemplated the task. "Tell me about it."

"In this report, we tie him to the group that funds his missions," David said in a whisper. "We want to expose them all."

"Tell you what," Gary said. "There's a dinner for attendees this evening. Why don't we talk there?"

"You got it, Mr. Wraithworth," David agreed happily. "See you then."

Gary walked back to his table. The show was opening, and the visitors soon poured in.

***

After a long day of selling memorabilia and signing autographs until his hand ached, Gary was anxiously waiting the close of the show at seven.

"Doin' okay?" Tera asked.

Gary rubbed his eyes and yawned. "Yup. Starving."

"Twenty more minutes," she said as she checked the time on her phone.

"I know."

"Are you sure about dinner here?" she asked for the third time.

"Yes," he answered and stood. The chair was becoming uncomfortable. "I'd like to find out more about these vids."

"I know you do. I'm uncomfortable with conspiracy theories."

Conversation halted as a pair of teenaged girls came to the table. Gary autographed one of their notebooks and sold the other a t-shirt. He waved at them as they walked away.

"I realize that," Gary granted. "I have to know more. David says there are more vids of this guy and that he's backed by big money."

"That's what worries me," Tera grumbled and crossed her arms.

"We don't have to stay long. I'd like to hear from Daisy to find out if it's legit."

"Okay, okay," she grumbled some more. "Just promise me that you're not going to let him know what room we're in."

Gary chuckled, but he could see she was serious. He agreed.

***

The Wraithworths wandered into a small banquet room a few floors up, set up to serve food buffet-style. A bar lined the far wall and beverages were free until nine.

Gary and Tera joined Daisy Hersh in the buffet line. The two women had not seen each other for nearly eight months. They shared a brief hug and slipped right into conversation as they loaded their plates with food. He joined them at a table in view of the double doors, and the trio began to eat and chat.

Nearly a half-hour passed before David Greely entered the room. He looked around for a moment before locating them and gliding over. His feet were barely visible beneath the overcoat.

David greeted them and removed the mighty coat, sending the scents of body wash free into the air. "What a day, huh?"

Daisy greeted him with a cheery hello, while Tera said nothing. Gary just nodded, his mouth full of food.

David went to the buffet and filled a plate with Italian beef, chicken, and bread. He set the plate down at the table and strode to the bar, returning with a can of cola. He sat next to Gary and across from Tera.

Greely dug into his food before he got into much conversation. David took his time eating and did so neatly, refusing to speak with food in his mouth.

"David," Tera started out when he finished his dinner. "You said that this man is responsible for more of these crimes? Do they involve famous people like Welks?"

"Some," he replied and leaned forward. "Do you recall the Ohio state representative that was running for governor in the 2016 race? Maxwell Jackson?"

Gary, Tera, and Daisy nodded, though it was Gary that answered. "Yes, I remember that. He was missing for about a week, then his car was found in a river. Am I right?"

"That's right," Greely said and casually looked around for eavesdroppers. "It happened less than a week after he announced he was running. I have a video made from a few security cameras that show a white SUV following Jackson's car after a stop for gas. In the gas station footage, our friend is seen sitting in the truck and watching Jackson."

"That's seems rather foolish," Tera commented. "How does this supposed professional hitman keep getting himself caught on camera?"

"It is pretty sloppy, but you have to admit, cameras are everywhere now," Daisy said.

David took a deep gulp from his soda. "That's all true, but evidence shows that he's acting with total impunity because of the organization behind him. Think of who has the power to command the erasing of evidence."

"What government organization would do such a thing?" Tera asked, sounding a bit annoyed.

"It doesn't *really* have to be a government thing, does it?" David asked with a sideways grin. "Not directly anyway. Big money talks and pulls the political strings, buying and selling politicians and getting their way. It's nothing new."

"I understand that, David," Gary said. "I have to say, I'm finding it hard to accept all this."

"Meaning what?" Greely said as his smile disappeared. "Are you saying those vids are faked?"

Tera's neck sprouted goosebumps. She wondered why David jumped to such a conclusion. She glanced at her husband and, catching his eye, read the same alarm bell. Daisy's expression seemed to agree.

"Not at all," Gary replied calmly. "What I am saying is that if I back this idea of yours and help publicize these crimes, I can't go in front of that camera and talk about political manipulation without evidence."

"I gotcha," David said and relaxed. "You don't have to. That report I told you about ties everything together."

"Okay," Gary said.

Tera looked from David to Gary. "You have to admit the targets are interesting," she said. "Other than Bellacosta, there are political ties to the rest of the victims. Welks isn't a politician, but he writes a lot of stuff that could gather a lot of negative feedback."

"Bellacosta isn't the only hooker to—" David began.

"I don't like the word hooker," Tera interrupted. "That was never proven in Mishka's case and a sex worker is still a human being."

"You're absolutely right, Mrs. Wraithworth," Greely offered. "I apologize. I'm saying that she's not the only non-politically motivated victim that we have video on."

"This 'we' you mention, how credible are they?" Gary inquired.

"That's myself, a few other YouTubers, a couple private detectives, and some law enforcement officers. All of which want to remain nameless outside of the report until this whole thing unfolds."

"Private detectives working for whom?" Gary pushed.

"One was hired by the family of Bellacosta," David explained and downed the rest of his cola. "Another is working for the parents of Ariele Trujido. Don't know if you remember her."

"Yeah," Gary said somberly. He had posted a video on his channel about her case less than two months ago. It was a sad story all around. Ariele disappeared from her home in the Chicago suburbs and the media-wide plea for help was made all the more urgent by the fact that her mother had developed lung cancer. Ariele was still missing and her mother passed away without ever knowing what happened.

"I saw your video…well, I've seen almost all of them, but that one was great," David said.

"I talked to her father before I made that video," Gary went on. "We spoke on the phone for a couple hours. His daughter missing, wife dying—"

Tera placed her hand on Gary's left wrist. He looked at her and smiled weakly.

"That must have been a pretty heavy conversation," Daisy commented.

"They're all pretty heavy," Tera said.

Gary's eyes widened. "Wait, you have video on her? Gray Hair's involved?"

David smiled at the nickname for the agent. "Afraid so. I'll send that to you next."

"How? All of it from the people you've mentioned?"

"I can't give up any names just yet, Mr. Wraithworth."

Gary felt both elated and angry. He looked to his nearly empty dinner plate. "So, what is your objective here, David? You and your colleagues want to catch these guys, you said."

"That's the idea."

"He can't be allowed to continue killing and abducting on behalf of rich elitists," Hersh added.

"Have you thought about this guy hitting back? Maybe making one of you disappear or worse?" Gary inquired gravely. He watched David's face.

"That's why I said I'd post the videos anonymously," David went on excitedly. "All I need from other YouTubers is that they make their own vids from that source. See? That way, Gray Hair's backers have too many targets to strike."

"Can't kill us all, huh?" Wraithworth said with sarcasm.

David shrugged, not knowing what to say. In essence, it was true.

Gary sat back and thought for a moment. He looked to Tera, who had that expression he was so familiar with. The one that told him she wanted to be anywhere but where she was.

It was obvious to him that Hersh was nearly as excited as Greely. She had been mostly quiet, but her eyes were keen.

"Tell you what," Gary said as Tera gave a sigh. "How about you show us the rest of what you have, and we'll talk about it?"

Greely gave them his winning smile once again. "You got it, Mr. Wraithworth."

***

David led the Wraithworths to his hotel room, just a floor below their own.

Tera was giving her husband the angry eyes and the silent treatment, but he felt he had to check out the remaining videos. Daisy had already seen the material and retired for the night.

David pulled a laptop out of a locked briefcase. It was a small computer, barely bigger than some electronic tablets, but the screen was bright and clear. David set the computer on the round table and clicked on the video he wanted.

"Now, this is the Maxwell Jackson vid. I have to pause…right…here."

The black and white video was grainy and soundless. The driver's window was halfway down and for a scant two seconds, Gray Hair's face could be seen.

In the moments that followed, Jackson could be seen getting in his car, an English brand of luxury sedan, and guiding it onto the two-lane road. The SUV followed a moment later.

The camera switched to another location that appeared to be a convenience store. It was color, though the night washed out much of it. Gray Hair was pushing the truck hard and gaining on the red sedan quickly. The two vehicles drove offscreen.

"They're headed southbound along US 23, and the highway turns to a four-lane," David narrated. "Jackson's car was found just north of the town of Delaware, Ohio. The official police report is that Jackson drove it into the water."

With that, David showed them stills of the crime scene. There were two wide, deep ruts in a muddy trail in between scores of trees. In the next shot, the ruts led to the edge of the murky green river.

"I don't know, David," Gary said after taking a close look. "I don't think that car of his was all-wheel drive. There are ruts in every direction except the last twenty feet or so. It looks like it was pushed."

"I tend to agree. And there are unexplained dents along the passenger side."

"Why not just blow up the car at his home?" Tera interjected. "To track this man down and run him off the road seems like…really hard to set up."

"I suppose they wanted it to look like an accident as much as possible," Gary surmised.

"But the lawyer…Schofield and Mayor Mackelby…they were shot openly," she went on.

"In all the discussions I've had with colleagues," David said, turning to Tera, "there are theories about that. Some say it's up to the member of The Council—as they are called in the report—to dictate the method of the assassination."

"And Gray Hair just does it?" she asked with a palm turned to the ceiling.

"He who writes the checks makes the rules," David said with a grin.

Tera gave him a half grin then rolled her eyes at Gary, who shrugged.

"You have to admit, David, this video is a bit weak," Gary said. "It's taken from multiple cameras of differing quality and the crime itself is absent."

"True, but the resolution is better on the originals and murderer and victim are on the screen together in both," the YouTuber said a little defensively.

"Are you sure of the locations of these places?" Gary tapped his finger on the laptop's touchpad, prompting the time display and highlighting the two security cameras.

"Definitely. They are within three miles of the spot where Jackson's car went into the river," Greely confirmed.

"And the police reports match up?"

"Yes."

"I'm sorry," Tera blurted, "but why hasn't this been blown up in the news? This is just the type of conspiracy theory shit that the networks would eat up."

"That's just the problem, Mrs. Wraithworth," David said. "There was some coverage when it happened, then poof! On to the next big thing. Online news sites pulled the articles they wrote on it. I saved the links when I was looking into it, but they've been deleted. Any evidence of them are screen printouts and URLs that lead nowhere."

To this, Tera's eyebrows shot up, her eyes did not roll this time, and her expression, as Gary read it, became one of intrigue.

The remaining three videos David showed were of the abductions of two teenagers. One was another runaway female with a story similar to Mishka Bellacosta's and the other was a boy from New York City. The boy was Anatoly Barekov, son of Feliks Barekov, a member of the Russian mob.

"That's a big story," Gary said. "The articles I read said the boy went home to Russia against his father's wishes, while the others proposed that he had been kidnapped by rival gangs."

"Then the trail goes cold and so does the news coverage," David finished.

"And again, no one's ever seen *that* footage," Tera added, pointing to the stilled image of Gray Hair dragging the teenaged boy to a van's open side door. The video had been recorded by a camera a good distance away, but the man was identifiable by his hair color and the shape of his shoulders and head.

The conversation soon became mired in details and, as all three were exhausted from the day, it was time to call it a night.

The Wraithworths returned to their hotel room and discussed David Greely and his videos. Tera was no longer apprehensive about dealing with the vlogger, but backlash from Gray Hair or his employers was still a concern. Their protection depended on the sheer numbers of the participants.

On this point, the two of them curled up in bed and fell asleep.

***

Gary and Tera had become so distracted over Greely's videos, that both had forgotten to set any alarms, either on the room's clock radio or their phones. The orange light of sunrise beamed through the narrow gap between the drapes. Gary tried to squint it away, but the sunrise insisted. After a few moments of denial, Gary blinked and focused.

"Shit," he grunted and sat up. He twisted to see the time on the clock, which was on the table on Tera's side. It was twenty minutes till nine. "Tera! Wake up! We're late!" he shouted as he jogged to the bathroom.

"Huh?" she grunted. The morning soon became obvious to her as well. She glanced at the clock, swore, and jumped out of bed.

The day was thusly set to a frantic pace, and by the time the couple arrived in the convention hall downstairs, the crowd was filing in. Gary was recognized by a few, and he told them politely that he was running late and to see him at his booth.

Once they arrived at their table and hurriedly set up, they could see that the crowd was not as heavy as Saturday. This was to be expected, and since they were late, it was a welcome fact.

The event was shorter on Sunday to allow the attendees to pack up and make their way home. As a result, the day passed quickly, and it became two in the afternoon before they knew it. The Wraithworths were due at the airport soon for their flight home.

Neither Gary nor Tera had seen David Greely that day, so as Tera packed up their remaining stock of t-shirts and caps, Gary took a walk to the end of their row.

When he got there, however, '*Greely's Reelz*' was packed up and gone. Only a few scattered cards remained on the white tablecloth.

"Pardon me," Gary said to the young lady of the next booth, who was also packing her things.

"Yes, sir," she said.

"I was wondering if you had seen David Greely…the man who had this booth?" Wraithworth asked.

"Oh, yes," she said. "He sold out of his t-shirts and whatever else he had, so he left…just after one, I think."

"I see," said Gary as he looked over her banner. She was a nature photographer that made videos of her travels. Many of her photographs were on display in frames. "Nice work," he commented.

"Thank you," she replied and did not try to feed him her spiel. She could tell from his event badge that he was an exhibitor.

Gary sauntered to the empty table and picked up one of David's leftover cards. It featured the t-shirt he was selling on the front and a description of his channel and media contacts. Gary pocketed it, returned to his table, and finished helping Tera pack. Soon, they were off to the airport and home.

Chapter Three

*T*he flight back to Minneapolis was pleasant and so was the drive back to their suburban home.

The days after TruCrimeCon went by slowly. While David had left their Saturday night meeting by saying he would email them once the first video was published on YouTube, they had yet to hear from him. In the meantime, Gary went on with his investigations and the preproduction for another cold case of a missing person was nearly ready to be recorded when Tera knocked on his office door.

"Yeah?"

Tera opened the door and poked her head inside. "Hey, which video is next?"

"The missing girl from Iowa," Gary answered. "The one that's been gone for seven years."

"Have you gotten any word from Greely?"

Gary cracked a smile, despite the somber material he was about to cover for his viewers. "Nope."

Tera sighed. "Okay, I was just wonderin'."

"I know. I am, too."

"Hey, comb your hair," she directed.

Gary pulled the handheld mirror from his desk drawer and checked. His hair was somehow mussed. "Thank you," he drawled and took his comb to it.

"Can't have my superstar lookin' shabby," she teased. She pulled her head out of the room and shut the door.

"Uh-huh," he uttered loud enough to be heard through the door and, having his computer and other material ready, recorded his video.

He stayed up late editing, as per his usual. The next morning, he uploaded it to YouTube and began the next one.

Such was life in the Wraithworth house and three weeks went by without a word from David Greely. Gary had kept up with the man's channel and he found that David was still posting about three a week, so he had not disappeared from the face of the Earth.

It was on the morning of the first Wednesday in August when Gary checked the email on his phone and found a message from an unknown address. Normally, Gary would have dismissed it as spam, but it was a string of numbers prefaced by 'dg'. He opened it and read:

All set on the first vid. Click the YouTube link below to view, or the one below that to download from FylShareNet:

Tera had already left for work, so there was no one to whom he could shout the news. He abandoned the preparation of his coffee and breakfast to scamper down the hall to his den.

He plopped down into his office chair and powered on his laptop. He found the email in his inbox and reopened it. This time, he clicked on the link to the YouTube video and watched. The channel name Greely had given it was *RydingtheRails*. There was only the one video for the channel and the followers were less than a dozen. He had titled it, "*The Killer Agent.*"

David had removed himself from camera and disguised his voice in a comical baritone to narrate the action. The video started out with the abduction of Mishka Bellacosta and Bill Welks. David went further, showing the murders of Mayor Thomas Mackelby and Martin Schofield, the attorney.

Gary cringed a little as he watched. He had not expected Greely to bundle so many cases in one video. Thinking further on it, he decided that David was right to do so, though it was a lot of information to throw out there at once.

The video lasted twelve minutes, with David going over the information on each case thoroughly, giving it a professional, yet campy quality, unlike his other channel's videos.

When it was over, Gary texted his wife, telling her that David's video was up. He then downloaded it for himself from the file sharing site. He found that David had not placed his narration on the file, making it easier for Gary to use.

Realizing he had not yet had his coffee, Gary went to the kitchen and resumed preparing that and his breakfast. He brought both back to the den and began gathering the research on each of the victims mentioned in the video. He would want to augment what Greely had included.

Collecting this information and organizing it took him through the morning and into the early afternoon. By two o'clock, Gary thought he had everything together and showered and dressed.

He began recording his off-schedule video, which would emphasize the importance of the subject matter.

"Good afternoon, *Wraithworks* fans, this is Gary Wraithworth and today, I'm presenting something highly unusual, to say the least."

Gary showed the video in its entirety, using David's pauses and highlights and filling in the case information as he saw fit.

He concluded with: "I have no idea who's running this *RydingtheRails* channel, but I think the videos speak for themselves. Why these cases have been virtually dropped by law enforcement I can't say. But I put it to you, the *Wraithworks* community to ponder and comment. Maybe we can get these cases back in the spotlight and find Bellacosta and Welks...and if we can identify this man with the gray hair, folks, we can bring him and his cohorts to justice."

With that, he signed off and stopped the recording. He watched it three times before deciding it was fine as is. The few places where he had misspoken, he had corrected on the fly, adding to the video's feeling of urgency.

He added the beginning and ending titles and posted the video. It was just after five in the afternoon.

***

Tera returned home from work soon after.

"Hey, come see something," he said after greeting her with a kiss. He grabbed her wrist and gently tugged as he began walking to his den.

"Wow, I had a great day, too, thanks for asking," she said as she was towed away. She giggled, caught up in her husband's excitement.

"Come here and sit," he said, directing her to his office chair.

"Okay, I'm here. Now what?" Tera asked, smiling ear-to-ear. She pulled the holder out of her shoulder-length auburn hair and shook it free.

"Just watch," Gary said and hit the play button on the YouTube screen. His video began to run and instantly, she was transfixed.

Tera maximized the window and leaned well forward to watch closely. When it was completed, she sat back hard and smiled.

"That was great."

"One take," he said.

"Oh, I can tell."

"Well, shit. Thanks," he said through a half-smile.

"It's okay, though. It worked," she said hastily. "It kept me interested and holy crap, Gary—" She trailed and pointed at the number of views.

"Yeah, that's the other thing. Eight hundred views and counting." He nodded and crouched next to the chair. "Followers have increased, too. Almost two dozen since posting."

"When did you post it?"

"Thirty-five minutes ago."

"No way!" She slapped the arm of the chair excitedly.

Gary smiled and nodded vigorously, like a kid who won the science fair.

Tera sat back and thought a moment. "How many other YouTubers are covering this news?"

"Hmm," Gary grunted and stood. "I don't know. Hey, have a look at David's *RydingtheRails* channel."

Tera tapped the laptop's touchpad, selecting the channel from the saved favorites. "Hmm...not even a hundred views."

"Okay, now search the name of the video," Gary requested.

Tera typed 'Killer Agent' into the search bar. She grinned when the *Wraithworks* video came in at the top of the list with Daisy Hersh's entry second.

Tera clicked on the videos listed below theirs and together, they were elated over the number of views theirs was receiving. The video, having been reiterated by fourteen other YouTube channels, had received nearly ten thousand views and was rising quickly.

"I can't believe it," Gary murmured.

Tera selected Daisy Hersch's video and let it play. Essentially, she had done the same thing Gary had, covering many of the same points, but her personality tended to be more chipper, as Tera liked to call it.

"Well, superstar," Tera said and grasped his hand. "Let's see if this thing goes viral. With so many people in on it this early, I can't see how it won't."

"Yeah," Gary said and sighed. "It's coming along just like David hoped."

Tera stood from the chair and the couple walked out of the den.

"It's going to go one of two ways," she said. "Either there will be a massive cover-up that shuts Gray Hair and his employers down or…there's going to be a shit storm of retaliation from our killer's handlers."

Gary stopped in the hall and watched his wife enter their bedroom where she would change out of her office clothes. He pondered her words. *What would it be? A cover-up or a shit storm?* His breath shortened when he realized that people could get hurt over this news. However, the bigger the story and the more people reporting it, the less risk there was for everyone involved.

He walked back to his den, sat in front of the laptop, and re-watched Daisy's coverage of the story. He could not help but envision the poor girl being cornered somewhere in a Denver alley.

He visualized her shrinking away in fear, tripping over a box of garbage, falling prey to Gray Hair.

Gary slammed his eyes shut and shook his head to make the picture go away. Worry settled into his chest, despite his usual optimism, and he wondered if he had done the right thing.

That night, his mind would not stop racing through the possible outcomes of his actions. After more than an hour, exhaustion overcame his restlessness.

<u>Chapter Four</u>

Gary rolled out of bed after nine the next morning, still exhausted. A hint of a nightmare remained, mottling his reality. As he shuffled to the bathroom, the cobwebs in his memory were swept away.

He noted the time on the bathroom clock. Tera must have realized he was having trouble sleeping and had let him stay in bed. He last recalled seeing the clock radio at ten minutes past five that morning before falling back to sleep.

He then went to the kitchen for coffee and breakfast. Tera had left him most of the pot and he poured a cup. Even though it was four hours old, the microwave breathed life back into it.

He thought of yesterday's video and was interested to see the statistics and to begin his investigation for the next case on his schedule. At the same time, he fought the feeling that a great beast had been unleashed.

Wraithworth went to his desk and opened his laptop. He drummed his fingers as it booted up, though it took only some seconds. He went to his YouTube channel.

"Holy shit!" he shouted and blinked, unable to believe his eyes. His Killer Agent video had earned well over fifteen thousand views and his subscribers had increased by ninety-three. He let out a whoop of joy and began to read the comments.

The number of 'likes' far outstripped the two 'dislikes' and set the tone for the conversation under the video. For most of them he simply gave a 'like', while others received his message of thanks. Others engaged him in questions, which he answered to the best of his ability.

As was his habit, he checked the views on his fellow YouTubers' channels. He did not view them as his rivals, as some did, but he felt that if he could gather nearly as many views as some of them, he was doing well. Daisy Hersh's views were over sixteen thousand, which made Gary smile. He had never been so close to her in any of the videos he had published which shared the same subject.

He then checked his email account and let out a whistle. He had received over a hundred messages since he had last checked.

Gary went to the kitchen for more coffee. Answering emails, especially so many, required eyes wide open.

He settled in and read his messages, taking them in chronological order and deleting the spam.

Gary had answered four of them, all fan mail which required nothing further than thanks and encouraging words. The fifth, however, stopped him cold. He set the coffee cup on the desk too hard and opened the email.

Mr. Wraithworth,

I think you remember me. I'm Mishka's mom. We talked a while in the weeks after my daughter went missing. I saw your new video last night. I don't even know what to say. Where has this evidence been? Why haven't our police investigated this man?

Please tell me what to do about this. I simply don't know what to do or who to talk to.

Rena

Gary sighed and sat back. His mind was utterly blank as he wrestled for what to say. He did indeed remember Rena Bellacosta. She was a single mother that had done what she could for her daughter, only to have her daughter leave home, end up working in a strip club, and eventually be abducted.

After several minutes, he formulated a reply in his head. He typed it out, only to revise it and revise it until, some fifteen minutes later, it made some amount of sense.

Rena,

I certainly do remember you. How could I forget? This newly uncovered evidence will reawaken attention to your daughter's disappearance. It will take some time, however. I know how ridiculous it is to ask you for still more patience, but I feel that patience is exactly what is required. I'm sure the police will have someone looking into this and all the other cases that this criminal is responsible for. I will keep in touch with you on this. I promise.

Gary Wraithworth

He sat back once again. After another moment's consideration, reached for the screen and tapped 'send.'

***

Over the next few days, surprisingly little more information came to light. The story had gained much popularity, being that Gary was now able to find many videos and even some news articles on the subject. His video always came in at least in the top five search results each time.

Ten days later, he found a video on YouTube that had been posted by a Pennsylvanian television news channel. It stated that the Thomas Mackelby case was officially reopened by Bloomsburg police. Greely's video was shown, stopping at the point where the mayor's bodyguard had been shot.

The next day, he found an online news article that proclaimed the Maxwell Jackson accident was now being investigated as a murder.

It came as no surprise to Wraithworth that the murder of well-to-do government officials received the most media attention. It always did, and that was just the way of things. He was disappointed to note that nothing new had come of Bellacosta's abduction and was shocked to find nothing on the disappearance of the author, Welks, other than a fan site's blog mentioning the video.

On Monday, August the fourteenth, he received an email from another address that included the letters 'dg' and opened it.

Hope all is well. Click the link for the next vid.

It was unsigned, and for a moment, Gary was uncertain. He had to admit to himself that echoing David's first video had left him feeling paranoid, especially after his YouTube channel was listed among the top sources for it, well above that of the *RydingtheRails* channel's original posts.

He tapped the link and played the video. David had chosen to highlight some other victims of the Killer Agent. This time, the security footage of the abduction of twenty-year-old Chicagoan Ariele Trujido was featured, along with the assassination of attorney Martin Schofield and a third victim, one who David had not mentioned in his conversation in Denver.

The sequence on this crime was just over five minutes in length, and it was taken from a gas station security camera across the street from a storefront mosque. It had been recorded at night, without color, and the only sound was David Greely's disguised voice as he narrated the scene.

"April 2016. Piscataway, New Jersey," he introduced.

A small white car slipped slowly into the frame from the right and parked two spaces away from a larger, dark-colored sedan, a type most often used by law enforcement. The driver, a young woman with dark hair, got out and looked around. To Gary, her body language was that of a person having come to meet someone.

David's narration continued. "This is Faiza Atiyeh. She was a freelance journalist. Her articles appeared in a great number of New Jersey, New York, and Pennsylvania news agencies."

Faiza stood next to her car while donning a hijab, a traditional Muslim woman's head covering. She moved to the sidewalk and looked about again before peeking through the storefront mosque's front door window. The lights were on, so she tried the handle. The door opened, so she went inside. It closed it behind her.

Nearly a minute passed, and shadows had begun dancing within the mosque's windows. A moment later, Gray Hair stepped out onto the sidewalk. He calmly walked to the large sedan, got inside, and quickly drove off screen.

"Oh, come on," Gary started. "What the hell did—"

With a mute violence that startled Wraithworth, the storefront glowed white and burst the glass into nothingness. Flames shot out of the open doorway and the window frame. The concussion shook the security camera.

"Faiza's body was burned badly, but dental records confirmed her identity," Greely's artificially deepened voice continued. "This camera footage disappeared from the files of the

Piscataway Police Department and the case was quietly abandoned for reasons unknown."

David followed the footage of her death with the display of several news articles she had written, focused mainly on the corruption that existed between the governor of New Jersey and the gambling and construction industries.

His narration finished with the question, "Was she silenced for her investigative journalism?"

Next, David covered the disappearance of a young woman Gary had covered on *Wraithworks* nearly a year before.

"Ariele Trujido was twenty-four years old. Her occupation? Escort."

"What?" Gary blurted in disbelief. He had covered her case himself and had found no evidence that she had been a sex worker.

The scene turned to a luxurious hotel lobby, adorned with comfortable-looking chairs and pillow-riddled couches. The video was crisp and in color. A man and a woman entered the establishment's front doors, walking closely together. Gary soon discovered that the woman was indeed Trujido, wearing an ornate evening dress and heels. The man she was with appeared to be old enough to be her father. He was tall, well-dressed in a suit that screamed money, and had well-chiseled blond hair and a handsome face.

"Shit," Wraithworth said.

"This footage is from the security camera in the lobby of the Renaissance Chicago. A hotel downtown," David continued. "The man in this footage is Tony Etchins, the son of oil tycoon Henry Etchins."

After a brief exchange at the desk, the couple headed to the bank of elevators.

"Note the timestamp. It is just minutes after ten p.m., the sixteenth of June 2016."

The color drained from the video and became grainy. Even so, the image of Ariele Trujido was clear enough for Gary to instantly recognize her. It was nighttime, and Ariele was walking through the parking lot. Gary recognized the location as the large retail store where she was employed at the time of her disappearance.

As she approached her little coupe, a vehicle rolled up behind her, coming within two yards before she turned around to see it. The headlights were off until her reaction, at which point, the driver turned on the SUV's headlights. Ariele kept her eye on the stalking vehicle, but kept her feet moving toward her car.

In a flash, the SUV came around her and cut her off. Ariele broke into a run, heading in the direction she had come. As Trujido reached into her purse for something, Gray Hair was on her and forced a white rag over her mouth. Ariele's struggles were short and her body went completely limp within seconds. Gray Hair dragged her to the SUV, tossed her in the back seat, and jumped behind the wheel. The SUV drove off, and the video ended a moment later.

"The date of her reported disappearance is nearly three weeks from the date of the Renaissance security video," David said. "Is there a connection between her sideline occupation as an escort and her client, Tony Etchins? Did The Council, the money men behind the Killer Agent, want her to disappear to protect him? Ariele Trujido is still missing, though given the Killer Agent's other missions for his handlers, it is not likely that she is still alive."

With that, the video ended.

For a time, Gary sat in his chair, trying to rid his spine of the tingling chill that had settled into it. He leaned back, and his eyes searched the ceiling as he contemplated his next move.

<u>Chapter Five</u>

*T*era returned home at her usual time, but Gary did not bring up the latest *RydingtheRails* video. He wanted to share it with her after dinner, along with the things he had found out that afternoon.

Gary helped put the meal together and as they ate, Tera noticed him staring at her with a strange expression.

"What?" she asked once she had swallowed a mouthful of chicken breast.

"Greely posted another vid today," he answered and took another small bite from his own.

"Really? Okay, so spill. What about it?"

"I think you need to see it after dinner."

Tera grunted with feigned annoyance. "Come on. Just tell me," she commanded.

"Nope." There was a lack of humor in his voice, but he was not morose.

"So, not what you were expecting?"

Gary shrugged. "Yes and no."

"Oh, come on!" she shouted and giggled.

Both sped through dinner and went to the den. Tera sat in Gary's chair and took over the laptop. She found the video and played it.

"An escort?" Tera cried once she heard David's description of Ariele Trujido.

"Just watch," Gary said from over her shoulder.

As she watched Ariele walk into the hotel lobby, Tera cussed loudly and paused the video. After a moment of close-up scrutiny, she sat back and looked up at her husband.

"What do you think?" he asked.

"I don't know about this escort idea. It just may be someone who looks like her," she said and gave a shrug.

"Maybe," Gary said. "Let it continue."

Tera watched the playback intently. When Gray Hair appeared on the screen during the abduction in the parking lot, she swore and shook her head.

"She's a little harder to make out in this one until she turns around," Gary commented and reached over his wife to tap the screen to reverse the video. "Right here," he said and paused it.

"Yeah. I see. The hotel footage just makes her look really different."

"I was thinking she used different makeup. Maybe more colorful."

"That might do it." Tera nodded and reviewed the hotel scene. "So, you haven't started your coverage on this one yet?"

"No." Gary sighed. "I was about to, though."

"Want me to stay and watch?"

"Sure." He walked around to the front of the desk to set up the camera. "If you think of something I should add, just hold up a finger and I'll find a spot to pause."

Gary began by setting David's video to play in the background over his right shoulder, began recording, and took his seat.

"This is another example of footage that the police should have in their possession. So, what's going on? How is it there is not enough evidence to find this man? Also, I have yet to investigate just what Faiza was working on at the time of her death, but I have to wonder why this Killer Agent had to take out an entire mosque just to get at one person. Was it to help cover the real reason for the crime? Did he, or perhaps The Council, have issues with Muslims in general? I don't know, but I am going to dig further into it, as well as the disappearance of Bill Welks, the author."

The coverage of Faiza Atiyeh switched to another case. Gary paused the scene with Tony Etchins and Ariele Trujido walking into the Renaissance lobby together.

"The second *RydingtheRails* story is about a missing person that we at *Wraithworks* covered here last year. To our surprise he says she's an escort. It was pretty unbelievable. However, after seeing this bit of video, I just don't know what to think."

Gary set his face to the upper left corner and Greely's video to fill the rest of the screen. He let it play to the point where the woman's face was quite clear and stopped it again.

"As you can see, it's a decent shot of the woman's face."

He placed the still in its own box and continued the video of Trujido's abduction. "This is newly uncovered as well, folks."

He paused when Ariele turned to the security camera. "She certainly looks like Ariele. It's pretty convincing."

He let it play to the frame where Gray Hair entered and paused it. "And... here's our abductor. Looks familiar, doesn't he? There's a really strong resemblance between the escort and Ariele's photographs. I'm thinking any difference might be due to lighting and makeup. I have a feeling, given these other videos by *RydingtheRails*, that it's legit."

Gary recorded more conjecture about the two cases then ended the video. He imported the footage into his editing software.

"Are you sure you should have promised an outcome?" Tera wondered aloud from the chair across from his desk. "We're not sure what we're dealing with here, hon."

"Tera, we have to do something," he stated firmly. "Everyone needs to see these vids. There's some big coverup or something going on."

"Hon, I know," she said quickly. She stepped to his side and placed a hand on his shoulder. "I have to tell you that this scares me a little."

"Well, it's a scary topic," he said as he sat back and looked up at her.

Tera nodded and gave a shrug. "Say, has our friend posted her video yet?"

"Daisy? I don't know, I'll check."

He searched YouTube for their friend's channel and, just as Tera had figured, Daisy Hersh's video was up. It was twenty minutes old and already had three hundred views. Gary selected it and they watched.

Daisy was more animated than usual. While talking to the camera, she had brought up a picture of Gray Hair from each of the *RydingtheRails* videos. Nearly in tears, she implored the police departments in each case to step up their efforts. As Gary had, she let the videos play in their entirety.

"Everyone, this man is a serial killer!" she exclaimed.

"Oh, shit," Tera mumbled. She had been wondering how long it would take for someone to use that term.

"He's a serial killer, and the men that are bankrolling him are terrorists," Hersh went on. "America is under siege."

"Yikes," Gary commented.

"If anyone has seen this man in person, speak out. Until next time, I'm Daisy Hersh and y'all stay safe and keep an eye out!"

The screen faded to black and her closing theme, a heavy metal tune from the 80s, played out to the end.

"Wow," Gary said and looked to Tera. "She was genuinely upset."

"She sure was," Tera replied. They knew Daisy Hersh long enough to know when she was acting. "I have to agree with her about the label. Gray Hair *is* a serial killer. So, you're going to post that as is?"

"I think so," Gary said and rubbed his chin whiskers thoughtfully. "I'm going to look into the Welks, Maxwell, and Atiyeh cases further. Perhaps even do exclusives on each of them."

Tera nodded and closed the door quietly on her way out. She went about making dinner, letting Gary work on his editing.

After a short break to eat, he went back to work on the video. He had it completed a short time later and the two of them tried to enjoy their evening, but thoughts of Gray Hair kept creeping into their minds. With their evening television shows watched but barely absorbed, they retired to bed.

The next morning, Gary posted his video. It was a day later than Daisy's, or even most other sites, but *Wraithworks* had a strong following. Within an hour, the new video had received just over a thousand views, proving to be more popular than much of his other work. By the end of the day, it was over ten thousand, more than half Daisy's views, and the same YouTubers that covered Greely's first post followed through to the second. Gary watched them all, and by the time he was done, he was convinced that the stories would go viral.

The number of views on his first video had almost doubled since he had last checked it, and when he searched the Internet on the Killer Agent story, he saw that many more news articles had been published, mostly by young, online-only publications. One of these featured an interview with New Orleans detectives regarding the abduction of Bill Welks. They had reopened the case. Another article confirmed that Dallas Police were reviewing the Mishka Bellacosta disappearance. Both were direct responses to the *RydingtheRails* videos.

Gary smiled, confident that the authorities would be able to identify Gray Hair.

<u>Chapter Six</u>

*I*t was late Friday afternoon, and his cellphone rang.

"Yes, sir," he answered and stretched in the hotel room chair.

"I see we've had multiple breeches in our security," the male voice drawled in a deeply southern accent.

"Yes, sir, but it's nothing we can't get past."

"I don't want to get past it. I want it dealt with."

"I understand, sir," the man answered. "I'm investigating it right now—"

"That's not good enough! I want each and every one of these sites shut down and I want to know the people involved and where they got these videos."

"Well, sir, if I may…shutting them down will do more harm than good at this juncture." He ran a hand through his thick, gray hair. "If we go in and start hacking channels, that's a clear message that we're onto them and I think that will send them running."

"So, what do you suggest?"

"I think this *RydingtheRails* guy is the one we're after. He's getting all this footage of me from the sources."

"These people were well paid for their discretion."

"Yes, sir. Very well paid."

"I am rather disappointed at all this."

"I understand, sir," the field agent went on. "I decided to track down one of those former assets and get a name."

"Do it. And please deliver my compliments when you see them."

"Thank you, sir. I certainly will."

"In the meantime, I will be having our friend shut down the *RydingtheRails* channel. At least for starters."

"Sounds good, sir." The call ended. He checked the time on the display and rose from the hotel room chair.

After waiting in the hotel room most of the day, it was finally time to get to work.

***

Payday always put a smile on Charlie Durand's face, especially when it was on a Friday. He stepped lightly from his old subcompact and let the door rattle when it shut.

He strode into his bank, check in hand, and in minutes, walked out with most of the balance in cash.

As he reversed his car into the street, someone honked. Instantly, his good mood was gone. He slammed his brake pedal down, leaned his head out of the window, and screamed obscenities at the other driver. In Charlie's mind, the other driver was always at fault.

"Dick," he called after the car he had almost backed into. "Yeah, you betta drive da fuck off."

Charlie thought to catch up to the other car, but he remembered the wad of cash in his shirt pocket. He watched the other car turn left as he approached the intersection for his right turn. He shrugged and moved on to begin his festivities.

He slowed down when he saw a New Orleans Police cruiser at the side of the road. It was a speed trap that he was familiar with, but he slowed down anyway. Knowing the officer behind the wheel by name, they exchanged waves.

Charlie drove on, away from the French Quarter and turned onto Earhart Boulevard, heading toward Metairie, an unincorporated section of Jefferson Parish.

In the late afternoon traffic, Charlie spotted an unmarked white Ford in his mirror. It had a spotlight mounted to the door frame on the driver's side. He turned north to see if the car would follow. It did.

Charlie knew that the department had two white Crown Vics left, so he carefully drove through the narrow streets, not wanting to do anything that would get him pulled over. The urge to drink was overpowering, so he kept on to his destination, turning west onto Route 61.

The unmarked car followed. Charlie began to sweat even more, compounding what the summer heat already drew from him. His ancient and rusting rice-burner's air conditioner had long ago broken. Durand kept his destination in mind and turned onto side street after side street, weaving his way to Metairie Road.

As he did, he considered that the white car might have belonged someone other than a policeman.

"Oh, God," he muttered and smacked his sunburned pink forehead with his palm. "Oh, God. Dey know what ol' Charlie done."

The white sedan was several cars and a large truck behind him. Charlie considered abandoning his evening's plan. There was no shortage of roads to turn onto, but he knew that not everyone behind him would follow. His car was slow, and the Ford would catch up to him quickly. The bar pulled at him as well, drawing him with the promise of a drunken Friday night.

After a few more blocks, the little dive bar next to the gas station came into view. Without another thought, Charlie tugged the wheel hard to the left, cutting it a little close with an oncoming car, whose driver had to brake hard and hit his horn.

Charlie Durand sloppily handled the old creaky Honda into a parking slot and cut off the motor before putting the transmission into park. This kept the motor from its tendency of running on afterward.

Charlie was sweating freely, breathing hard. He could hear his heart pounding in his ears. He threw open the door and jumped out, fighting the urge to glance at the road. He strode to the bar's front door.

Just as he reached for the handle, he caught the reflection of the white sedan in the door's rectangular window. The car continued along Metairie Road.

Charlie yanked the door out of his way and headed for the nearest barstool. He watched the door as he sucked down his first beer and a shot of whiskey. The bar was busy, but that was not unexpected for a Friday evening in New

Orleans. By his second beer and shot, his focus on the front door faltered.

As the evening went along and the sun dimmed, more people filtered inside the tiny bar. Conversation filled the long rectangular room, and despite the ceiling fans and relative darkness, it remained uncomfortably warm.

By his fifth beer and shot, Charlie had also downed two glasses of ice water. Nothing helped keep the sweat from dripping down his back.

Why did I ever help that fool? Why'd I keep that damned video?

He looked around and did not see a friendly face. All were strangers except the bartender, a tall, youngish man that was slow to serve the likes of Charlie Durand. It was the female patrons he preferred to attend. For that, Charlie did not blame him.

It became late, so Charlie paid up, leaving little tip and headed to the restroom. People seemed to watch him as he staggered past.

Durand pulled up to the urinal and let his rented fluids free. He stared at himself in the mirror while he washed his hands. He looked unclean, used up, and old. He ran water through his sweaty, thinning salt-and-pepper hair, but it did no good. He stood there for a moment longer, knowing full well he should not drive home.

"At least I know dat much fo' sho'," Charlie said to no one.

Two others stumbled into the men's room, and Durand took the open door as an invitation to leave. Without a word to anyone, he walked out the front door, intent on sleeping in his car.

The hot and humid night air was no relief. He slowly stepped along the sidewalk in front of the mini-mall in which the bar was snuggled. Charlie stopped in front of his hatchback and leaned back against the building. He tilted his head back to rest against the brick and closed his eyes. The world began to reel and, when he opened them, he glimpsed something white on his left.

It was the Ford sedan, parked under the streetlight. Charlie swore and, without thinking, stepped away from the wall and toward his car. It was night and the Ford's windows were tinted, so he could not determine if it was occupied.

"Oh, no," Durand said in a panic. "Ain't gonna get Charlie. No, sir."

Fright ignited his adrenaline, Durand turned to get into his car, more willing to be pulled over by police than to face who he thought belonged to the white Ford.

Charlie let out a short yelp when he realized his way was blocked. A tall figure in a suit stood in the way and far too closely.

"Who da fuck−?"

"You remember me, Durand," the man stated. The voice was familiar, smooth and almost musical.

Charlie stammered and took a swaying step back.

The suited man closed the distance in a blink and the next thing Charlie saw were stars and blackness. He was lying on his back and then there were hands around his throat. He struggled but could not breathe.

"You kept that recording we told you to make disappear," the man in the suit said. "Then…you gave it to someone and now it's all over the Internet."

Charlie's vision partially returned, allowing him to focus on his attacker's face. It was the gray-haired man, the one that had come to him to destroy the dashcam video.

"I want a name, Charlie," he grumbled in his face.

Durand tried hard to capture air, but the hands had a vice grip. With his vision darkening again, Charlie tried nodding.

"Yes? You have the name?"

Charlie nodded again.

The man in the suit lessened his grip on the tiny man's throat. "I'm listening."

"David," Charlie said and gasped for more air. "Greely."

The big man's lips grew apart and Charlie could see teeth. He supposed it was a grin.

"David Greely," he repeated. "Good. Now, where may I find him, Charlie?"

Chapter Seven

Gary awakened Saturday morning and found himself alone in bed. He had been up late the previous night, working on Monday's video. He did not post to his channel on the weekends, though he did some editing or research when needed.

He got out of bed and found his wife snoozing in her favorite spot on the couch. A full cup of coffee sat on the table next to her. She had the television on with the volume low.

Gary turned and went to the kitchen. He prepared his own cup of coffee and retrieved his cellphone from the counter, where it had recharged overnight. He powered it on and dropped it into the front pocket of his robe.

Being careful to not awaken Tera, Gary quietly set his coffee cup down and took a seat in his chair. He did not bother to reach for the television remote. The cartoons she had fallen asleep in front of would be just fine.

Gary took a sip of his coffee as the cartoon went to a commercial. He dug his phone out from the pocket and began paging through messages, which knew no schedule. Emails, direct messages on social media, and new likes and followers on YouTube came in at all hours.

He checked his channel for view counts, especially those regarding the Killer Agent. He was happy to see that they were quickly becoming his most popular videos.

He reviewed a few of his colleagues' pages and found the same. When he looked for the *RydingtheRails* channel, he found that David's posts were gone.

"Shit," he whispered. He rechecked his email and found nothing from either address Greely had used, nor was there anything from a new email address with a 'd' or a 'g' anywhere in it. He checked his spam folder and found nothing.

Gary sipped more coffee, contemplating what it could mean. He got up and went to his den, retrieved his laptop, and returned. He quickly verified that the videos were indeed gone.

He opened his email and began to type a note to Greely's main email address, the one attached to his *Greely's Reelz* channel.

David,

It was fantastic to meet you at TruCrimeCon.

Gary stopped and chewed his lip in thought. Perhaps it would be better to not contact him.

He selected Daisy Hersh's address and began typing.

Daisy,

Have you noticed the RR videos are missing this morning? I wonder what happened.

GW

Gary only had to wait a few minutes for a response.

Gary

Yeah not good. The channel's gone too. Have you called him?

Daisy

"What?" he squeaked. He searched YouTube once again. The standard YouTube note that the channel was suspended for violating site rules popped up, accentuated by the slanted smiley face.

"Holy shit," he whispered. Switching back to his email, he composed the reply to Hersh.

Daisy

What on Earth is happening? Also, I don't have his number so I can't call him.

Gary

By this time, Gary had paced the living room while downing his coffee, waiting for his computer to chime its notification. With his cup was empty, he strode back to the kitchen for another.

As he stood at his counter, his cellphone sounded off in his robe pocket. The email from Hersh read simply:

Can't get him here either. What now?

Daisy ended the single line with an emoji expressing concern and tears.

"Shit," Gary mumbled. "Good question."

He returned to the living room as Tera was waking up. They exchanged 'good mornings', but she could tell something was wrong. When she asked, he explained the situation.

"Shit," Tera reiterated. "Does he live alone or with his parents?"

Gary snapped his fingers and simply pointed at his wife. She smiled, as it was a gesture that showed his approval of the idea. He typed a quick email to Daisy and they waited for her response.

As they did, Tera retrieved her cellphone from the kitchen, where it had been plugged in to recharge. She retook her spot on the couch and launched the internet browser.

"Damn it. You're right. The channel is gone."

"You doubted me?" Gary asked tensely.

"It's not that. I just had to see for myself. You know how I am."

"I'm going to send David an email to his original address," Gary said. "I started one but didn't send it."

"What are you going to say?" she asked.

"It's just a 'nice to have met you' message. Nothing revealing. Just something to start a conversation. If he answers it, then he's all right."

Tera nodded. "Good idea."

Gary finished typing the email that he had started earlier and sent it.

The reply from Daisy came a moment later.

David lives in a suburb of St. Louis. I and another friend of his are trying to see if someone has a number or something.

Daisy

"Okay, well, the ball is rolling at least," Gary said and explained Daisy's email.

"I'm sure he's fine," Tera said. "Maybe he'll answer the email."

"Hope so."

***

The rest of Saturday went by. The Wraithworths spent it handling errands or relaxing, but David Greely's situation was still on their minds. They went to bed that night, restless and worried. There had been no update from Daisy, but they had refrained from following up. Gary knew she would keep them informed.

***

Gary woke while it was still dark. He rolled over and intended to drift back to sleep. He thought of David Greely, however, and could not relax. With a heavy sigh, he rolled over onto his back and began to stretch.

He soon realized that he was hopelessly awake. He tossed the blanket from himself and got up. He shuffled to the bathroom then went to the kitchen to retrieve his phone.

"Come on," he murmured as the phone booted up. Once it did, he checked his email. "Yes!" he exclaimed. Both Daisy and David had replied after Gary and Tera had gone to bed. He tapped David's to read it first.

Mr. Wraithworth,

It was nice seeing you at the con. We have to get together on that project we talked about. It's a little more involved than I thought. I'll be in touch soon.

David

Gary read Daisy's email next.

Gary

I got a number for David and called him myself. He says the videos were taken down by someone who hacked the account, but YouTube pulled the channel. Maybe someone complained? He says he will be creating another channel and make another video today. I guess we have to wait. At least he's okay.

Daisy

Gary let out a breath and stared at the last line again. "For now, anyway," he said.

When Tera woke up, he told her the news. She was relieved as well and settled into her morning by helping her husband prepare breakfast. The two of them sat in the kitchen and ate their eggs, bacon, and toast in quiet contemplation until Gary spoke up.

"David said our special project is more involved than he thought," he added.

"What do you think that means?"

"I think...*he* thinks that someone might be looking for him. Think about it. He probably saw that his vids were pulled first and then...sometime shortly after that, YouTube shut the channel down."

"Considering the subject matter, that would make me damn nervous," Tera concluded and took another bite of her eggs.

"That's what I'm thinking."

"So, what do we do?"

Gary accessed YouTube from his phone and checked his videos. His channel was still active, and all his videos were still up. Those featuring Gray Hair's crimes were still there and gathering views.

"I hope Daisy can get his phone number so I can call him," he said quietly. "On the other hand, that might be too direct."

"The emails you've exchanged might be enough to give him away," Tera said offhandedly.

"Shit. You think?"

"It's possible," she said and shrugged.

"The guy who hacked into his channel could also hack into email accounts," Gary said, working it out as he went along. "We would never know about it."

"But, hon," Tera said more soothingly, "David's been careful. He's been bouncing around from wi-fi source to wi-fi source, probably even using a network that disguises his IP address—"

"Like Tor," Gary inserted. Tor was an acronym for 'The Onion Router', a browser that connected the user to the internet by sending it through a maze of networks, disguising the user's web address.

"Exactly. Like Tor," she agreed. They were getting ahead of themselves and she knew it. After delving into so many cases of murders, abductions, and even some government conspiracy capers, the paranoia had become easy to cultivate. "Listen, hon. He's been smart, not even including his channel by joining in on the re-broadcasting he has asked all of us to do. There's no way this FBI guy can find him."

Gary nodded. As they came to know David, his intelligence had been evident. They had to believe he was safe.

***

The Wraithworths went about their usual Sunday chores. He mowed the lawn and mopped the kitchen floor while she went out for groceries. All the while, Gary kept checking his email and text messages for something from Greely.

The heat of the day took a lot out of Gary. He showered for a second time that day and decided to take a nap. When he awakened at 3:30, he reached for his cellphone, lying on the nightstand and found an email notification. The message was from another 'dg' address:

I found this today. Mr. Durand was the man that came to us with his recording of the Killer Agent dressed as a LA State Trooper. I guess the shit has hit the fan. More soon.

Underneath that was a link to YouTube and another to FylShareNet. Gary preferred to watch such things on his laptop, but as he was comfortable where he was, he let it play on his small screen.

It was a newscast from a New Orleans local television station. The anchorman was speaking, with a picture of a man over his shoulder. Under the picture was the name 'Durand.'

"Authorities are looking for suspects in the killing of a part-time police department employee that was found strangled Friday night in his car, outside a bar in the Metairie neighborhood. Charles Durand of New Orleans had worked for the department for over nine years."

The scene cut from the newsroom to the parking lot of the bar. A single car was surrounded by yellow police tape and the building and street reflected the flickering of a collection of flashing blue and red lights.

"Police have been questioning residents and business owners in the area in an attempt to find witnesses," the anchor continued. *"They are encouraging anyone that may have seen anything*

relating to this crime to step forward as they have no leads at this time."

"Holy shit," Gary mumbled and jumped out of bed. He waved at Tera, who was sitting on the couch, watching television.

"Hi−" she started.

"You gotta see this." He held the phone out to her.

She took it and played the video. At the end, she shrugged. "That sucks, but who is it?"

"Oh!" Gary blurted. "Sorry, just woke up. Anyway, David sent that to me in an email."

"So, he's all right?" she asked.

"He is, but he says this Durand guy was the one that gave him the video of Welks being abducted by Gray Hair in the phony Louisiana State Trooper suit."

"Really?" Tera thought a moment as her husband stared at her for a reaction. "Crap. This isn't good."

"That's what I was thinking," he agreed. "So, I think I'm going to do a special *Wraithworks* episode on it. I start−"

"No!" she interrupted.

"What?"

"No...don't make any more of these damn videos," she pressed. "We need to step back. Cover the usual stuff."

"Tera," Gary said in a lowered volume, "this is an important lead. We can't just ignore it. There's a whole conspiracy going on."

"I don't know about that, Gary." She took a deep breath, and then flipped her auburn hair from her face and fixed him in place with her pale blues. "We're getting caught up in something over our heads, here."

"Tera—"

"Gary, a man's been *killed!* What the hell have we helped to stir up? We got into this stuff, trying to cover missing persons cases...to help people. Now look!"

Gary sat on the couch next to her and turned quiet a moment. She had a point, of course, but the force inside him that wanted to bring justice had intensified with the addition of this new video. He took a deep breath and let it out slowly as he carefully thought out his response.

"This Durand guy is just one in a whole line of victims, Tera," he said as he held her gaze. "Gray Hair is involved in some horrific crimes and he's got the backing of... this Council. They even have people on the inside of the FBI."

"What if he...or they come after us?"

"We'll have to handle it."

"*Gary!*"

"We're not the only ones out there risking ourselves to bring this to light," he pushed on quickly. "Look, my vids are already out there. I think the worst they are prepared to do is knock the channels off YouTube. There are almost twenty other people covering Greely's story. It's almost viral, Tera."

"I believe in shining the light on the evils in this world, Gary," she said in a calmer tone. "It scares me to think that Gray Hair has this power to kill indiscriminately. But what if he shows up at our door?"

"We call the police, I guess. What anyone else would do."

"That's fine, but by then it might be too late."

"I know. Tera, I think to back off now is a mistake," he said adamantly.

Tera sighed heavily and gazed back at the television. "Okay, well, go make your video then," she said and shooed him away. The worry lines in her forehead were prominent.

Gary leaned over and gave her a long kiss on the cheek and went to his den.

As he downloaded the video onto his laptop, he found that David had indeed created another channel. This one was called *RydingtheRailz*, with the 's' changed to a 'z'. David again disguised his voice as he narrated the vid, telling the full story of the murder and making the accusation that Durand was killed for having turned over the Bill Welk's abduction video.

Gary shot his video, featuring the audio clip of David's revelation. Once he was done editing the piece, totaling a mere five minutes, he found himself hesitating to post it.

He checked Daisy Hersh's channel. She had nothing new on the Killer Agent. Three of the other YouTubers in the rebroadcasting scheme had fresh videos, also featuring Greely's item about Charlie Durand.

Gary read the news articles he had found and noted them in his video. It all made sense. Durand had been an employee of the New Orleans Police Department according to four news agencies, two of them from New Orleans.

After more deliberation, he hit the 'upload' button and was committed. If it was a discovered that Greely's accusation was disproven, he would retract it. A couple of minutes later, the video was added to his channel.

Wraithworth sat back in his office chair and contemplated the possible repercussions. He shook his head to clear it, remembering that it did no good to dwell on such things.

Gary closed his laptop and rejoined Tera.

Chapter Eight

David sipped his coffee leisurely as he watched the cars pass by the café window. The place was busier than he had hoped for, and the conversations hummed away around him, making it hard to concentrate. It was a Sunday, after all, and it appeared that most of the customers had dropped by after attending church. Many were very nicely dressed. The ladies in the room were too fancifully decorated to be grabbing a beverage before heading to a job somewhere.

Greely refreshed the screen on his laptop. He smiled when the '1' appeared next to the *Wraithworks* channel. It indicated that a new video had been uploaded.

"Took ya long enough, Gare," he said under his breath.

He placed his wireless headphones on his head and clicked on the video. He smiled as he watched it. Like his other three friends, Gary had kept the audio clips from his video. It was fine with David, as he liked the strange and creepy voice he had chosen to disguise his own.

He had driven all the way from his suburban home in Eureka to the little town of

Pacific to use the café's wi-fi. He jumped around from town to town around the St. Louis area to make sure his identity was safe before he uploaded anything to his channel and FylShareNet. YouTube could censor him all they wanted, but he knew as long as he had friends like Hersh, Wraithworth, and the others, the Killer Agent story would get out.

Greely smiled as a shiver went through his body. He felt terrible for Charlie Durand but working against The Council and their hired gun gave him a good feeling.

David's imagination conjured the thought that a book deal, a television miniseries, perhaps even a movie would come out of his hunt for the Killer Agent. Bringing down the criminals may pay off well enough to finance his way out of his mother's home. He ran his free hand over his short-cropped hair and downed the remainder of his coffee. He could not remember ever feeling more in command of his life.

David put his laptop into his backpack and left the café.

It was a warm day, and the gray clouds above threatened to rain once more on his way home. He cared not a bit. A feeling of invulnerability permeated him as he walked to his car, a rusty white 1989 Beretta. He had not bothered to lock it and dropped himself into the seat. The starter cranked slowly, reminding him that he would need a new battery soon.

He pulled out into the road, turning homeward. The radio had broken many years ago, leaving David to the gargling sound of the V-6, the squishy-whir of balding tires, and the wind. The old car bounced and shimmied awkwardly over bumps, and the worn steering mechanism forced him to make many corrections at the wheel.

David's smile was indefatigable, however. Things were going to change for him when this was over. The world would be rid of a powerful gang of criminals and he would have notoriety, money, and maybe even a girlfriend. He would move out of his mother's house, maybe even relocate to Los Angeles once the movie took off.

He imagined himself behind the wheel of a new car. Maybe a Camaro, or a Mustang. *No, screw that. A Mercedes!*

After winding his way through the light Sunday traffic, he eventually made it to his home on Drewel Court in Eureka. He pulled into the driveway and parked his old oil-burner behind his mother's sedan.

As David pulled himself out of the car, his eyes fell on a white Ford sedan. It crawled along the street and turned into a neighbor's driveway.

The blood drained from Greely's face as the memory of Faiza Atiyeh's death flashed through his mind. Her killer had been driving an unmarked Crown Victoria.

The tinted windows kept David from seeing inside, but his imagination struck down the positivity it had planted so well and froze him in place with panic, leaving him leaning on the open car door.

"Oh, shit," he said over and over as energy seemed to ebb from his knees. Seconds went by with every beat of his heart. No one got out of the Ford. It sat there in his neighbor's driveway, just out of earshot, so he could not tell if the engine was still running.

David forced his legs to work. He slammed his Beretta's door and strode to his home's front door. Miraculously, his shaking hands guided the key into the lock and turned the knob in one motion. Once inside, he spun and closed the door, pressing his forehead against it. He pressed his face to the crescent-shaped window and watched the Ford.

It just sat there, and no one got out.

"Oh, shit," he rambled again. "Go 'way…go 'way…bastard, go 'way."

"Davy? What is it?"

Startled, he let out a shout and spun around. It was his mother. He let out a rush of air and closed his eyes.

"David!" she called and came in from the kitchen. "What's going on? Are you high?"

"What?" he hissed, trying to breathe. He felt faint. "No…no…I'm not, Ma."

"Drunk then," she pressed in a tone of disappointment. She placed her fists on her hips and blocked his way past.

"I'm not…would you please stop!" he shouted.

She brought herself inches from his face and was, searching his eyes. "Yeah, well, okay. You're not. Honestly, I have no idea what your problem's been lately." She turned and headed to the kitchen. "You've been acting squirrely for over a week."

"Sorry," he said and looked back through the window. The Crown Victoria was gone.

"I have to go to work in a little bit, so I made you some stew for dinner."

He looked to the left. The Ford had traveled to the end of the cul-de-sac, turned around and was cruising slowly the other way.

"Fuck," he whispered through clenched teeth. David ducked his head from the window, crouched, and quickly put distance from himself and the door.

He turned up the hallway and went to his bedroom. Staying low, he went to his window and pulled the thick blue drape back. He saw the tail end of the car slip around the corner and out of sight.

David let out another breath of relief, but the feeling was short-lived. He thought of Durand once again, and the whole scenario came to him. The Killer Agent found the New Orleans police employee and made him confess to handing over the video to Greely rather than destroying it like he had been paid to do.

Come on. Think about this. How many millions of those Crown Vics have been built?

David would not allow these rational thoughts to dissuade him. "No. No…that was *him.*"

He left the window, sat at his desk, and opened his laptop. He launched his Tor browser and began writing an email to everyone in his list of YouTubers.

Guys,

I think I just spotted the Killer Agent. A white Crown Vic parked up the street and rolled by the house real slow.

Any suggestions????

dg

Greely hit 'send' and sat back in his chair, keeping it turned toward the window where he had a good view of the street. There was no sign of the car.

A knock on his door startled him to his feet. "What?" he squeaked.

The door opened part way, and his mother's head appeared. "Sweetie? I have to go to work. Can you move your car?"

David let out a breath that he had not realized he had been holding. "Be right there."

She went out, leaving the door open. David went to his window and looked both ways. The white Ford had not returned.

David went out front to move the Beretta. He waved to his mother, who was already in her car, waiting for him.

***

He parked the Crown Victoria around the bend and angled the driver's side mirror so he could see if Greely was leaving. There was only one way out of the neighborhood.

He picked up his tablet and connected to the camera he had placed in the Greely home just an hour before. A clear view of his subject's open laptop was dead center. He smiled and tapped the screen to select 'Capture.' The enhanced still picture revealed the email addresses of Greely's co-conspirators. The agent saved the shot and sent it to his cellphone. He was not in the least concerned that the email was about his car being spotted by the subject. In fact, it made him smile. He wanted them all terrified.

He selected a number from his contact list, sent the picture, and then made a call to that same number.

"Kenny," he said, "I just sent a pic to you. I need the YouTube channels belonging to those addresses shut down."

"Just a moment," the bored voice returned. Kenny Anderson had been in the hacking business for a long time and often said it was no longer a challenge. "Got it."

"As soon as possible."

"Understood, Del," Kenny answered. "I'm on it."

Just as the call ended, the tiny import that belonged to Nancy Greely drove by. Using his tablet, he accessed the camera once more.

David had returned, taking up almost the entire frame. He was sitting sideways in the office chair, appearing to be looking through his bedroom window, which to the camera, was at the extreme left and out of view.

Del Hampton grinned. His appearance had the desired effect. The clever YouTuber nervously ran his hand over his face every few seconds, and his eyes danced as he constantly checked his window.

Del grinned and counted the hours to sundown.

***

Gary's cellphone gave a short chirp, indicating a new email had arrived. He took his feet from the deck's picnic table and reached for the phone. He read the email and swore loudly.

"What?" Tera said from the other side of the table. She put down her novel and looked at him with concern.

"Greely just sent an email. He says that he's being stalked by someone in a white Ford."

"Oh no." Her eyes widened in fright for their new friend. "Well, tell him to call the police."

"I am," Gary answered as his thumbs did the typing.

"How in the world did they find him?"

"I'm guessing that this Durand fellow was tortured for the information before he was knocked off."

"My God, Gary," Tera said in a shaky voice. "What the hell have we gotten into?"

Gary shrugged, not knowing what to say this time.

For several minutes, Gary and Tera sat on their deck and contemplated in silence. Unable to concentrate on her book, Tera placed a bookmark and set it on the table.

A few minutes later, the ringing of Gary's phone startled them both. Tera let out a short cry.

"Hello. David?" Gary said into his phone.

"Mr. Wraithworth." Greely sounded frightened out of his mind. "I haven't seen him at all. I mean…I did, I guess, being that it's got to be his car. Who else can it be? It has to be *him*, right?"

"Slow down, David," Gary said. "Don't panic. Maybe…maybe it's not even Gray Hair."

"I thought about that, but I have a bad feeling that it is−"

"Okay, well−"

"−I mean it has to be. I've never been in trouble with the cops or nothin'. He's here to kill me, Mr. Wraithworth!"

"David, just stop and take some breaths."

"Yes, sir."

"And knock off the 'Mr. Wraithworth' and the 'sir' stuff. 'Kay?"

"Uh-huh. Okay."

"All right. Now, what's your living situation? Are you in an apartment?" Gary looked at his wife. She was following the conversation intently.

"I live with my mom," David said, sounding defeated over having to reveal the truth. "We're in a ranch home."

"Okay. Well, you have a car, right?"

"Yeah, kinda."

Gary raised an eyebrow at that, but let it go. "Well, get your mother and go to the police station. You'll have to tell them everything."

"She went to work," David said. "I'm all by myself. We're in a cul-de-sac situation here. I've got one way in and out by car."

"Shit," Wraithworth mumbled.

"Yeah."

"David, you'd better call the cops, then."

"You think so? What do I even say? 'The dude from the YouTube vids is after me?'"

"Tell them you see a suspicious vehicle in the neighborhood," Gary suggested. David said nothing, but his breathing was fast. "Listen to me. It's hours until nightfall. Do you have friends you can call? Maybe go visit in a public place? Take 'em to a bar, maybe."

Greely was hesitant to answer. "Um... I'm not old enough to drink. Not for another two months."

"Oh!" Gary answered and smiled. "I had no idea, David. Can you get to a friend's house?"

"Not really," David admitted morosely. "Most everybody I know is online."

Gary looked to Tera. She shrugged her shoulders at her husband, wanting to know what was happening. He held up his index finger and nodded.

"David, I don't want you to panic," he said.

"I'm not. Yet."

"It may not even be him, you know."

"It is. I know it is."

"David. Just remain calm. Do yourself a favor. Get out of the house for a while. Go to a mall. A public place. Anything."

"Yeah. Yeah, I think I'll do that."

"Okay. Good man. Call me if you can, but please get to the police."

"Sure. Thanks, Gary," David said.

Gary ended the call and explained what had occurred.

"What do you think? Is he being paranoid?" Tera asked.

"He's beyond just paranoid, but I think he has reason to be. He's scared out of his mind."

***

Hampton heard only Greely's side of the conversation, but Wraithworth was mentioned. The call had ended and now Greely was preparing to leave, shutting the laptop and stuffing it into his case.

Del shut down the tablet and dropped it onto the passenger seat. He started the car and waited. There was no way out of the neighborhood without Greely driving past him. In a few moments, the rusted Beretta came into his view and stopped at the intersection.

Del watched as Greely jumped on the Chevy's accelerator around the right turn, the only way out of the labyrinth of cul-de-sacs.

Hampton smiled, put the transmission into drive and followed.

***

David zig-zagged his way out of the neighborhood and made a left onto Bald Hill Road. He floored the gas pedal, kicking all six cylinders in the guts and leaving a puff of bluish-white smoke behind him.

Bald Hill was a two-lane stretch of rural throughway, passing between Eureka's little league baseball fields, thick trees, small businesses, and more residential land.

David found himself quickly catching up to a pickup truck doing just below the twenty-five mile-per-hour speed limit. He cussed and tapped the brake. The Crown Victoria grew large in his rearview mirror.

Greely crossed the double yellow line and looked past the pokey truck. He jerked the wheel back to get in his lane to dodge an oncoming car.

Immediately, blue and red lights filled his mirrors and his ears were blasted with a warbling siren.

"Shit!" David shouted. Doubt flowed through him and he considered the possibility that the Ford's driver was actually a policeman.

David slowed as the siren whooped two short blasts, then let out one long one. There was no shoulder, so he pulled over shy of the stop sign at Dreyer Street.

He looked from one mirror to the other and reached for his wallet. He pulled the parking brake lever and let his foot off the brake pedal. This left his car in gear, but completely still and with the taillights out. This would look like the car had been put in park.

Seconds ticked by, and David felt his eyes sting from the sweat trickling down from his forehead. He blinked and wiped it away. When he looked into his sideview mirror again, the driver of the white Ford had gotten out. The door shut, and David angled his head to see the man, expecting and hoping it would be an officer in uniform.

Instead, the man walking slowly up to the Beretta was wearing a medium-blue suit. The supposed police officer stopped as if to look around. David saw that he was tall and could not see his face.

David reached out to his mirror and touched the top with his fingers, aiming it upward and bringing the man's head into view. He seemed to lock eyes with David, even though the man wore sunglasses. Just as David's mind registered the familiar gray hair, the man removed a gun from his shoulder holster and resumed his walk toward the Beretta.

Shit! It's him!

Breathing hard and fast, David went into a panic. He dropped the parking brake and mashed the gas pedal.

A heartbeat later, the air was filled with immensely loud pops. The rear window exploded, and lead rounds pierced the trunk lid and roof pillar.

Greely screamed as he spun the wheel to the right. Glass and bits of metal flew about the cabin of the coupe. The front right tire spat out thick white smoke and David fought to bring the steering wheel back to the left.

More bullets struck the passenger door's window and dashboard, flinging pieces of glass and plastic into David's face. Loud metallic knocks sounded as the body panels were hit.

David held the pedal down. With the worn-out V-6 screaming, he flew past the businesses on Dreyer. His cheeks and arms stung where debris struck him.

Just ahead, Dreyer terminated into South Central. He stomped on the brake pedal with both feet, forcing it nearly to the floor. The dry-rotted tires screamed and smoked, while pedestrians halted to watch the scene unfold.

The white Ford was again in Greely's mirror as he made the left turn.

Chapter Nine

*I*t had become evening and the Wraithworths had not heard from Greely. Gary had busied himself by preparing dinner on their charcoal grill and having a cold beer. His concern for their friend had kept him from enjoying anything. His imagination ran freely, and none of the visions of Gray Hair's confrontations with David Greely favored the YouTuber.

Tera saw the torment in her husband as he stared into space while grilling their burgers. He would check the time on his cellphone frequently, and he paced in front of the grill.

To settle her own nerves, she had opened a bottle of wine and tried to enjoy it while she cut up the vegetables for their salad. A tear came to her eye when she remembered their first meeting with the man she had learned today was not even old enough to drink alcohol. She had been almost mean to him they day they met and now he might very well be in danger.

Gary and Tera sat down to dinner, and no conversation passed between them. Gary took a great forkful of salad into his mouth, sighed heavily, then glanced at the clock on the wall.

"I say we call him if we haven't heard anything by seven," Tera suggested. She looked to her husband for his agreement.

"I was thinking more like six."

"That works for me," she said and tried to smile.

Gary checked his phone many times for texts and emails, but there was nothing from Greely.

Wraithworth returned to his deck after eating and counted the minutes to six o'clock. With a last check of his email, he called David's cellphone. After five rings, the voicemail activated.

"David, it's Gary. Just checking on you. Give us a call, okay? Bye."

***

Del Hampton wiped the sweat from his forehead with his handkerchief. He was breathing heavily as he climbed up the embankment from the depths of a burning grove of trees.

Greely had proven to be a difficult one, leading him into a chase on Highway 50, then onto Lewis Road, a curvy country two-lane drive. It was only a matter of time, however, as the old Chevy's brakes faded, and Greely lost control of the car in a steep left curve. The Beretta struck tree after tree on its way down the hill.

Hampton had jumped out of his car and slid down the grassy surface to make sure his deed was done. As he approached the burning Beretta, it exploded, and the fire quickly spread to the dry foliage it had landed upon.

Del reached the Crown Victoria and jumped in. Before he gathered any further attention, he switched his police lights off. Noticing that the black smoke was building fiercely, he threw the car in reverse, turned around, and sped away.

**

Gary's face paled as he thumbed through YouTube via his cellphone. The videos were gone, replaced by the words along the top of the screen: *This account has been terminated for violating YouTube's community guidelines.*

Wraithworks was gone.

For a long time, Gary could not bring himself to move. He stared out into the trees that lined his back yard. The number of hours he and Tera had spent on the channel was incalculable.

He pulled himself out of his chair and shuffled into the house, aiming for the den. He sat behind his laptop and doublechecked. In a moment his laptop confirmed what his phone had told him.

Gary rested his head in his hands, wondering what to do next. What was worse than the channel being gone was the fact that it was no coincidence and not a computer glitch. Greely was being hunted down by a killer and now his own channel was suspended. He wondered if he and Tera were next on the killer's list.

Wraithworth tapped the screen to switch to Daisy Hersh's channel.

"Shit!" he exclaimed.

Hers had been terminated as well.

"What's up?" Tera said from the doorway. Gary showed her that their channel and that of Hersh's were removed. Her face went white. "Oh, shit."

While Tera watched, Gary tapped on a few of his favorite channels, focusing on the people that had joined Greely's cause. One after the other, he discovered each of their channels terminated. He found only three YouTubers out of the twenty-one that had featured videos on the Killer Agent remained.

"Quick, Tera," Gary said excitedly and pointed to the screen. "Take down these addresses and send them a warning. Make sure they've made backups of their videos."

Tera typed away on her cellphone. In a matter of two minutes, the messages were sent.

"I think I'll call Daisy," Gary said. "Maybe she has some phone numbers for those last three." He initiated the call with the speakerphone on.

"Hello," she answered on the first ring.

"Daisy—"

"Gary! What the hell is happening?" Daisy shouted. She had discovered her lost channel.

"We sent emails to Rup Williams, Trish Talbotz, and the channel called, *Destabilize the System*, whoever's running that one," Tera said from over Gary's shoulder.

"I know the numbers for Rup and Trish," Daisy said. "*Destabilize* is run by a real young kid. I met him a few times at cons. Mickey...or Mikey something. Don't have a number for him."

"Can you call those two?" Gary asked. "Just give them a heads up and have them recruit some fellow YouTubers to help cover this stuff."

"I will right now," Hersh said.

"Let me know what happens. 'Kay?"

"Sure. Bye."

Gary sat back in his chair and rubbed his stubbly face in both palms.

"Now what?" Tera whispered, as if to herself.

"Well, I'm thinking that I'm going to make a video and create another channel to upload it."

"You think that's wise?"

Gary took his hands from his face and looked up at his wife. "We can't let this injustice go unchecked, Tera."

"Injustice? Gary, it's just a YouTube channel," she said and came closer. "Think about poor David—"

"Shit! David," Gary blurted, forgetting that he was going to keep trying to call him. He tried again, but it went to voicemail. This time, he did not leave a message.

"I wonder if he already got your earlier message," Tera said.

"I can't tell, Tera. He can't or won't pick up."

"I think we need to call his mother. Did you get a home number?"

"No," he answered. Using his laptop, he entered David's full name and the town of Eureka into a search engine. He found two families in the St. Louis area by the name of Greely. The first one was a male name, the second was a Nancy Greely. David had said he lived with his mother, so Nancy was the prime candidate. Knowing that his cellphone's battery was running low, Gary picked up his landline and dialed.

"Damn," he hissed when there was no answer. He tried David's cellphone again. After a few rings, his call was routed to voicemail.

"What do you think we should do?" Tera asked from the doorway.

Gary scratched his chin whiskers in thought. "I don't know. Let me try the numbers a few more times."

Agreeing, Tera went to the living room to watch television.

Gary prepared to make his video, but then, thinking about it, he stopped. He turned his attention to his laptop and brought up YouTube again.

Wraithworks was still shut down, as were the other channels, excepting those last three. For a time, he stared at the ceiling, fighting back his urgency to get his channel reinstated. He was in the same predicament as some other high-profile YouTubers, so he did not feel alone, but the helplessness was still present and gnawing.

His laptop gave a short bell sound. A new email had arrived. Checking it, the sender's address seemed familiar.

It was Mishka Bellacosta's address.

"What the—?" To confirm it, Gary opened the email folder he had labeled 'Bella', which contained every email correspondence on the missing woman's case. He sifted through emails from her mother, her father, and the detectives that had been on her case, those forwarded to him from the parents, and even some from Mishka herself to her mother before her disappearance.

Gary compared the address to the one of the newest emails in his inbox. It was identical.

"Tera!" he shouted toward the open door. He heard her steps pound through their hallway.

"What? What happened?" she called to him before she even entered.

"Look at this," he demanded and pointed to his screen.

"Oh, that's bullshit!" she declared and crossed her arms. "Open it."

Gary shrugged and did so.

Mr Wraithworth, where I am now is better. You will like it too

Mishka

"That's the worse damn joke I've ever witnessed," Tera decided. "Her father sent it."

"No...why would he?"

"Okay, maybe not her father. Maybe a friend of hers that thinks impersonating the missing or—well, I hope I'm wrong, but—presumed dead, thinks this is funny."

"I don't know, Tera," Gary said as he read it again. He compared the new email again to the old one from Mishka to her mother, then to another older one she had written to a friend. "In almost every email, she signs it with 'Mish', not 'Mishka'."

"So what?"

"So, whoever sent this is trying to scare us and never bothered to research the girl to know her habits."

Tera ran her hands over her face and gave her short curls several light tugs. Something she did when she was thinking.

"I don't like this, Gary," she said and folded her arms.

"Neither do I," he replied and closed his laptop.

Chapter Ten

*D*el Hampton sat in a diner's booth, calmly waiting for his dinner order while he watched police cars, a fire truck, and an ambulance roll by, all taking the turn onto Lewis Road. He smirked and made a call from his cellphone.

"Yeah," greeted Kenny Anderson.

"It's me. So, what did you do?"

"I used the Bellacosta girl's email to deliver a message to Wraithworth."

Del could not help but let out a laugh. It was hearty, loud, and dark. The sound of it turned many heads and gathered looks of apprehension. "Did he reply?"

"No. Don't really expect him to," said Kenny. "I'll monitor the girl's account for a while to see."

"That should rattle the prick," Hampton rumbled. "Do me a favor and send Wraithworth's info to me. Address, their cars, license plates, the whole bit."

"I've already been putting that together. They're in Eden Prairie, a suburb of Minneapolis."

Del grinned. "Great. Send it all."

"What's next?"

"Looks like I'm heading to Minneapolis. Tonight," he replied.

"Long drive. Wouldn't it be better to fly?"

"I want to stay off airport cameras for a while. Have you tapped their phones?"

"Yeah," said Anderson. "I'll call you if something interesting comes up."

"That's fine," Del said more quietly. "Do me a favor and email Wraithworth again. I have a message I want you to deliver."

***

The Wraithworths spoke at length throughout the evening about their next course of action.

Gary had called David's cell four times throughout the night without result. He tried the residence of Nancy Greely twice more as well, but there was still no answer.

Daisy Hersh phoned just as Gary and Tera prepared to turn in for the night. Gary spat out his toothpaste and snatched the phone from his pocket.

"Gary," Daisy greeted. "I've talked to Rup and Trish and they have their videos backed up. They've also reached out to some YouTube friends that'll share the story."

"Can I send them my videos to help?"

"Of course," Daisy agreed. "I'll forward their emails to you. I've sent them links to my vids of the Killer Agent story, too. If nothing else, showing our stuff will be a sort of protest to YouTube."

"If they did it."

"What do you mean?" she asked.

"Well, I was thinking about it," Gary said as he paced his hallway. "Our Killer Agent vids disappeared first, right? The rest of them were there."

Daisy gave a thoughtful grunt. "That's true. The rest of my videos were still up for a while, then the channel was suspended. I emailed support right away."

"I did, too. You didn't get a reply, did you?" he asked. He entered the bedroom and sat on the bed. Tera listened intently.

"No. I don't expect a reply until tomorrow."

"Tell her about Mishka's email," Tera whispered.

Gary nodded to his wife, and said to Daisy, "I still can't get Greely on the phone."

"No? Hmmm," Daisy said. "You know, Gare, we've either been doing this too long or we're onto something."

"I think you're right on both counts," Gary said with a worried smile. "Um… there's something else, too."

"What?" asked Daisy. She sounded apprehensive, as if she were unwilling to take on any more weirdness for the day.

"Okay, well… I received an email from… I'm guessing some sicko, using Mishka Bellacosta's email address."

"No fucking way!" Hersh shouted.

"Um…no. Seriously."

"What did it say?"

"The person pretending to be Mishka said that she was happy where she was and that I'd like it there, too."

"Holy shit, Gare," Daisy uttered. "Maybe you and Tera should think about taking a short vacation somewhere."

"With everything that's happened, maybe you're right," said Gary. "Maybe David will answer his phone in the morning and there'll be a good reason for all this. I'll let you know what we find out. Okay?"

"Hope so. Goodnight," Daisy said.

Gary wished her a goodnight in return and the Wraithworths went to bed.

***

Del's phone rang then stopped. Awakened, he opened his eyes slightly. It was still dark beyond the car windows, so he decided to check his voicemail later.

The cell rang again moments later. He mumbled a string of profanity and pulled the phone from his pocket.

"Yeah."

"Del. It's Ken."

"Yeah. What?"

"I thought I'd call and let you know I sent that email."

"You could have told me later," Hampton returned.

"Stopped for a nap, huh?"

"Yeah," Del said. The dashboard clock read 3:13. He had slept for two and a half hours.

"Where are you?" Kenny asked.

"A rest stop in Cedar Rapids," he replied and looked around. There were three other vehicles in the parking lot and no signs of people.

"All right. Also, you should know that Daisy Hersh called Wraithworth last night," said the hacker. "They let it slip that they have a few more YouTube buddies out there that are planning on re-uploading the Hersh and Wraithworks episodes."

"Didn't get 'em all, huh?"

"Nope," Kenny admitted. "Now I know who they are, and I'll take those three down in a little while."

"Good. Thanks," Del replied.

With the call ended, he got out of the car and stretched. He retrieved his small suitcase from the trunk and walked inside the rest stop's main building. In the men's room, he was alone to wash his face in the sink and change his clothes in a stall.

Refreshed with a large cup of coffee from the vending machine, he slipped back behind the wheel, pulled out of the parking space, and re-entered I-380.

***

For hours, Gary drifted in and out of a paper-thin sleep until he gave it up just after six that morning.

He walked to the kitchen, made a cup of coffee and stopped at the bathroom on his way to the den. At his desk, he opened his laptop and checked his email.

Gary sipped at his coffee and coughed when he saw another email from Bellacosta's hijacked address. He opened it.

Gary

They are coming. Just welcome them and they will be merciful.

Mishka

Gary stared at the words for several minutes and wondered what to do. He lay his head back in the chair and closed his eyes.

Some time later, Tera poked her head into the den and gently called his name. To her, it appeared that her husband had nodded off in his chair. The moment he heard her voice, his eyes opened and dispelled the notion that he had been sleeping.

"Hey. Come here," he bid and waved her in.

"Good morning to you, too," she said and stepped to his side. She read the opened email on his laptop. "Holy shit."

"Yeah."

"Okay, no kidding," Tera said as she placed her hand on his shoulder, "I think we might need to call the police."

"Possibly," he replied and sighed. "I'm going to check on Greely again."

"I'll get some breakfast started," Tera said and went to the doorway. "Eggs?"

"Yes, please and thank you," Gary answered. He powered up his cellphone and waited for it to awaken. As he did, he went through the rest his email. There was fan mail, much of which contained concern and questions about the reasons for the channel's disappearance, but nothing from Greely or any of his alternate addresses.

Next, he brought up YouTube. He cussed sharply when he found that the channels run by Rup Williams, Trish Talbotz, and *Destabilize the System*, were all gone. After running several searches using 'Killer Agent', and the names of his victims, he found only two videos. They were both from channels run by news services and did not have 'Killer Agent' in the title but had set them as keywords. One featured the story on the Bill Welks disappearance and the other was the murder of Thomas Mackelby.

Gary ran through the contact list on his phone and redialed David Greely's cellphone. It went to voicemail without ringing. Checking the time, it was not quite seven a.m. It was early, but the situation was too urgent for politeness. He then tried the number for Nancy Greely. This time, someone picked up. A female voice, trembling with worry or sorrow, greeting him.

"Hello, is this Nancy Greely?" Gary asked.

"Yes, who's this, please?"

"My name is Gary Wraithworth and I'm looking for David Greely. Have I reached his home?"

A sharp sob came through the phone's tiny speaker and his heart sank.

"I take it that you're his mother," he ventured in a gentle voice.

"Yes," she said. "Are you from the police?"

"No, ma'am," Gary replied and quickly explained. "I'm a friend of his, I guess you'd say. We both have...or had... channels on YouTube."

"Oh," Nancy Greely said, thickly disappointed. "Well, I'm not going to talk about what happened, and I think it's in poor taste that you call my home so soon afterward!"

"Wait, please." He had the feeling she was about to hang up. "I apologize, but I have been trying to reach him. Has something happened?"

"Don't you watch the news?" she nearly shouted into the phone.

"I haven't had the television on this morning, Mrs. Greely."

Nancy Greely could not respond past sobs.

"Is he okay?" Gary asked.

"He wrecked…his car," she finally managed to say. "It burned."

Gary hesitated. "Was he…run off the road?"

"They don't know for sure," Nancy said. "Went off the road they said, down a hill−"

She fell silent and Gary closed his eyes. He could not even imagine her pain. "I'm terribly sorry. I met him in Denver for TruCrimeCon."

"So, let me ask you something, Mister…I'm sorry, what was the name?"

"Wraithworth," he answered and spelled it.

"Just what was my son mixed up in?"

"I'm not sure I can explain," Gary stammered.

"How 'bout you try?" Mrs. Greely demanded. "My son is dead, and I want to know what the hell happened! He crashed his stupid old car on a road he had no business being on! Now you call me less than an hour after the State Troopers left and tell me he just met you? Talk to me, Mr. Wraithworth."

At the mention of David's death, he shuddered. "Well, he and I and a number of other YouTubers were investigating a serial killer and abductor," he said.

"Go on."

Gary went on to describe the previous day's events. David's call, Gray Hair's stalking of him, the murders, the abductions, everything. He spoke uninterrupted and when he finished, there was silence.

"Are you there?" he asked after a moment.

"Why didn't you tell him to call the police?" Her voice was strained, and she sounded as if she were speaking through clenched teeth.

"I did. I promise you I did," Gary returned mildly. "He said he was on his way to the police. I tried calling all evening. I looked up your number and I tried that, too."

"I work nights."

"I didn't know that," Wraithworth said lamely. "I don't know what to say, Mrs. Greely. I can't tell you how—"

She ended the call without another word. At that moment, Gary wished for the days long past when someone could slam down the receiver into its cradle. The electronic click of disconnection lacked significant release for the grief that Nancy had accrued, and he felt the need for some sort of penance, no matter how slight.

He set his cellphone down on the desk and sat back, staring at the far wall, lit as it was by the morning sun spilling beyond the drapes.

At some point during the conversation with Mrs. Greely, Gary had become aware of Tera's presence in the doorway. It was not the first phone call that had been filled with emotions as a result of their work on the *Wraithworks* channel. Grief was shared, stories traded, and tears were shed on both sides.

Gary was not startled by her hand falling gently onto his shoulder. Instead, he reached for it as if he had seen it coming.

"Breakfast is ready," Tera whispered in his ear.

Gary nodded and patted her hand. He knew without asking how much she had overheard. She took him by the hand and led him to the kitchen, where he went through the motions of eating his eggs and bacon.

The news on the kitchen television droned on. There was a story about a solar eclipse to happen that day, but it received little attention from the Wraithworths.

The next story made Tera gasp. Gary followed her gaze.

On the small screen set upon the counter, a young female field reporter stood in a two-lane road that was closed due to the fire trucks and police cars behind her. Beyond them, a blackened forest land spewed white smoke.

Tera grabbed the remote and raised the volume.

"...*brought under control in the dead of night. A car belonging to a Eureka woman, Nancy Greely, driven by her son David, went off the right side of Lewis Road, where it burst into flames and started this small forest fire. Authorities have determined that the car itself, a 1989 Chevy Beretta, was only identifiable by the license plate, which had fallen from the car on its way down the hill.*"

Tera turned off the television once the story was over. "No wonder they can't ID it. There's nothing left," she murmured and wiped away a tear from her cheek.

Gary sighed heavily and pushed himself from the table. He stood and took his empty plate and fork to the sink.

"What happens now?" she asked as she watched him cross the floor.

"I guess I'll shower," he said. "Maybe when I get out, I'll have an answer."

***

Gary dressed in his black *Wraithworks* t-shirt and gray cargo shorts. He had chosen the shirt in defiance of the channel's termination and had decided to go ahead with the appeal video and send it to YouTube. He was determined to bring it back online.

Tera slipped into the bathroom and from his chair in the living room, he could hear the water running. In the meantime, he wanted to see if there was more about Greely's accident anywhere on the news. He doubted it, as the only reason such an item had made it to the national news was the small forest fire that had ensued.

It was just before eight as Gary reached for the television remote. The morning sun reflected sharply off something on the street, stinging his eyes. He turned the television on and stood, curious to see what was outside. As he reached for the curtain to draw it, his eyes found the source of the reflection.

A white Ford sedan was parked up the street. The paint shone in pearl-white brilliance while the windshield and chrome grill scattered the sunlight. The rest of the car was in the shade of the neighbor's tree. He could not determine if the driver was inside.

The remote dropped to the carpet with a muted thump. Without a thought, Gary yanked the curtain to the center, cutting the light in the room by half.

Holy shit, he's here! Gray Hair is here!

Gary Wraithworth turned to find the cordless phone. It was not in the living room. He dashed up the hall and banged on the bathroom door as he passed it. "Tera! Get outta there!"

He had turned and entered the den by the time she replied from behind the closed door.

Gary snatched the phone from the desk and ran back into the hall. He knocked on the bathroom door and opened it. The room was warm and humid from the steamy shower.

"What the hell is going on?" Tera called from behind the curtain.

"It's him. Outside," Gary answered. From his standpoint, he could see both the front and the back door of his home. He looked back and forth frantically.

"Who?" she asked and shut off the water.

"Gray Hair," he replied. "His car's out front."

"Oh, come on, Gary!" She slid the curtain back and stepped out. She took the towel from the rack and began drying.

"I'm serious," he insisted. "His car is here. The one David Greely described."

Tera curled her lip and glared at him as she continued drying. "Ford made millions of those white cruisers, Gare."

"Yes, I know, but Greely said Gray Hair was driving it… casing his house."

"That was just yesterday," she said as she dressed. "He drove overnight to come up here…for us?"

"I know that's a long way, and I know how common the car is, but I have a feeling–"

"I think we've been making these crime vids too long," Tera interrupted and tugged her t-shirt over her wet hair. "Your paranoia is getting to you."

"Fine. That's fine," Gary retorted. "You just go have a look out the living room window. He's parked next door under the neighbor's tree."

Tera rolled her eyes and shoved past him. She strolled to the front room window and tugged the curtain out of the way. Gary followed, looking over her shoulder.

"No one's inside. Honestly, though, we must see a dozen white Crown Vics every time we leave the house, hon."

"Look, I know it's a longshot–"

"And you feel terrible about David," she filled in. "I know." She reached to him and took his hand. "But it looks like it's a detective's car. I can see the light bar along the top of the windshield."

Gary approached the window and looked out. The wind had shifted, moving the shadows from the tree branches. Tera was right, there was no driver and the red and blue strobes were clearly visible.

"I can see that," he said and dropped the curtain back in place. "He's still with the FBI, Tera. I'm sure he has the authority to use those."

"Hmm."

***

Del Hampton snickered. From his place in the bushes across the street from the Wraithworth residence, and with the help of his miniature binoculars, he could see them in the living room window, sneaking peeks at his car.

He picked his phone from the inner pocket of his suit jacket and touched 'redial.'

"Hey," he said into it quietly. "Have you cut them off yet?"

"Yeah, I coordinated everything and they're offline," replied Kenny.

Hampton could tell that Kenny was beginning to share in his excitement. Soon he would have the Wraithworths frightened nearly to death.

"Great work," Del said. "I'll be heading inside in a few."

"Cool. Good luck," wished Kenny.

Del ended the call without another word and dropped the phone into his pocket. He pulled his 1911 from his holster and quietly cycled the slide to put a round into the chamber. He set the safety and returned it to its place.

He watched Tera Wraithworth with his binoculars for another few moments, knowing he would have to move soon. Several cars had driven by since he had taken his position, and he had no idea if the family that resided in the home next to him was inside. He was prepared with the normal cock-and-bull story and his phony Minnesota State Police detective's badge in case he was discovered.

Del watched Tera pull the curtain closed and, with a quick glance around him, stood and jogged across the street.

***

"We can call the police and report a strange vehicle in the neighborhood," Tera suggested.

"I was thinking just that," Gary replied. "Maybe we can–" He pressed buttons on the cordless phone but stopped and frowned.

"What?"

Gary held the handset out to her so that she could read the message on the display.

Check Landline

Tera tested it by hitting the 'talk' button and putting the speaker to her ear. Gary saw the skin at her cheeks go whiter and her eyes widen.

"Nothing," she declared. "Just use your cell."

He ran to his den, grabbed his cell from the desk and rejoined his wife. A circle with a diagonal line through it told him the bad news.

"No signal," Gary growled. He checked the connection to their Internet. "No wi-fi, either!"

"What? How is that even possible?" Tera asked angrily. She looked at his cellphone and saw he was right. "Let me check my phone. It's in the kitchen." She turned and walked briskly up the hallway.

Gary shook his head and pulled the curtain away further. Looking up and down the street, he saw no one and the world outside appeared absolutely still.

Chapter Eleven

Del made his move once the Wraithworths dropped the curtain and slipped from his view. He had no idea whether they had discovered their loss of communication with the outside world, but he had no intention of dragging out his task.

He crossed the narrow street, walking calmly but purposefully. From behind his aviator sunglasses, his eyes constantly searched for residents. It was Monday, so most people would be on their way to work. At that moment, the only sound was a dog barking.

Hampton broke into a brief jog when he stepped onto their blacktopped driveway. Reaching the garage, he scrutinized his surroundings. He grinned at his luck and moved toward their front window. Quickly, he walked in front of it on his way to the front door.

He noted the rectangular windows set into the wooden inner door and focused his sight there for movement. There was none.

Del placed his hand on the screen door's handle. It came open with a gentle tug. The hinges were nearly silent.

He took a chance by placing his face closer to the glass. All he could see was a small foyer, decorated with wedding pictures on the wall and a wooden table with a green, vine-like plant sitting upon it.

Hampton read the engraving on the door's locks and knew the name to be one of a competent manufacturer, though mid-grade in quality. He gave the knob a try and found it locked. With his left hand, he withdrew a small leather case from his jacket pocket. He opened it and removed a small lock-picking rod. This he inserted into the bottom of the lock and left it while he removed his snap gun from the case. In the place of a barrel, a long, thin pin had been fashioned.

Del steadied his gaze on the foyer beyond the window, inserted the snap gun into the lock and pulled the trigger three times while putting pressure on the small rod he had placed at the bottom.

The lock turned.

The sound of a car approaching made Hampton slip into a practiced feign. He pulled the snap gun from the lock and held it in his right hand, straightened to his full height and made the motion of knocking on the door with his left. To appear casual, he tapped his foot, as if waiting for a response.

In the reflection of the door's windows, Del watched the shape of a black, full-sized SUV glide along the otherwise quiet street. Del hastily replaced his lock picking tools to his jacket pocket.

Seeing no movement within the home, he opened the door and went inside. Like the outer door, the inner made no sound other than a faint swoosh along the thin throw rug.

Hampton closed both doors behind him, barely allowing the sounds of the latches to click. He stood still while he listened and pulled his pistol. All he heard was his own breathing.

He took several steps forward until he could see the entire living room. No one was there. Del frowned and held the 1911 out in front of him. Silently, he dropped the safety.

An archway across the room led to the bathroom and two bedrooms. Each of the doors were open. He gave them a quick look and found them devoid of life.

He stepped back into the living room and ventured down the hallway. The first door on the right was also open. Within it, he found a desk, a few chairs, and a camera tripod without a camera. A few of the desk's drawers had been left partly open.

Moving on, the kitchen was gloomy, having only the sunlight screened by the partially opened blinds. It was filled with the aroma of coffee and bacon.

Hampton turned and found a small guest room at the rear of the house, also empty. Beyond that was the laundry room, which was still and silent. Having decided his presence had somehow been discovered, he abandoned his attempts to move about stealthily. He re-entered the bedrooms, though this time he whipped open the closet doors.

Hampton moved back into the living room and opened the door to the attached garage. Inside was the Wraithworth-mobile, a dull, mid-sized sedan. The car was empty.

He jogged through the narrow hallway yet again, this time finding the door to the back porch. It was open.

Looking out, he caught a glimpse of movement near the property's back fence. He yanked his mini-binoculars from his pocket and found it again.

Turned to look back, but not seeing Del in the shadows of the unlit room was Gary Wraithworth. Ahead of him ran his wife, Tera.

"Well, shit," Del mumbled and bolted for the front door.

***

Gary helped Tera over the four-foot-tall wood fence. He watched her land feet first, only to drop onto her butt. He climbed over and helped her up.

"Come on," he urged and adjusted the camera bag on his shoulder.

Tera let out a short burst of profanity as he wiped the moist dirt from her jeans. "I hate to say this, Gare, but your paranoia better pay off this time. I just bought these jeans!"

"Nice. For now, just go, will you please?"

Fuming, she took to a run toward the next street. Her purse, hung cross-body, slapped her hip with each step.

Gary took a glance over his shoulder but saw no one following. The pit of his stomach vibrated with tension and fear. He followed his wife through the neighbor's yard and past the little blue cottage. Tera reached the driveway, stopped, and turned back to him.

"Now where?" she panted.

Gary had no answer. He knew no one on Hillside Drive, the street to the west of their own. The police station was not far, just on the other side of Scenic Heights Road, the intersection of which he could see from where he was standing.

"Gare!" Tera shouted and ran the way they had come. She grabbed a handful of his *Wraithworks* t-shirt.

"What the−!" He stumbled after her, rounding the corner of their neighbor's little blue house.

"It's him," Tera explained once they were in the shadows.

Gary then heard the airy sound of a slow-moving car. He dared a peek around the corner in time to see the Ford sedan rolling by at walking speed. For a moment, the urge to pull out his camera and record the scene seemed a great idea, but a moment later, the car was too far away.

Gary straightened up against the wall and looked to his wife. "He saw us leave the house."

Tera checked her cellphone. "I've still got nothing on this thing. Gray Hair works for powerful people if he can cut off our phones. We've got to get to the police station."

"Okay. Let's cut through the yards."

Gary walked in that direction with Tera following. Together, they stayed close to trees and in the shade. As they were both wearing dark clothes, he thought it to be an advantage.

Some of their neighbors had not put up fences, so reaching Scenic Heights Road was easy. The presence of traffic emboldened them to walk along the road in plain sight, though they did so briskly and on the lookout.

They crossed the street after more than a block, entering the driveway to the fire department. The Eden Prairie City Center was just beyond it. The big building housed City Hall, the community center, and the police department. The police were on the south side of the building.

Neither of them slowed, but Gary breathed a sigh of relief and Tera smiled.

The short blast of a siren right next to them startled Gary and Tera, and they froze. It was the white Crown Victoria. The passenger side window was down, and Gary found the barrel of a large handgun pointed at him. Beyond that was the scowling face of Gray Hair himself.

"Get the fuck in the car," he growled at them. "In the back. Now. Or I'll shoot you both where you stand."

For a moment, both Gary and Tera remained still. "Uh…look−"

"Shut up 'n' get in this car!"

Tera, to Gary's left was the first to move. She reached for the door handle and opened it.

"That's right," Gray Hair said. Once Tera was partly in the car, Gray Hair turned the gun on her. "Follow her in and close the door, Mr. Wraithworth, or I'll take her head off."

Gary followed instructions and took a seat next to Tera. They clasped hands tightly and Gary could feel Tera trembling at least as much as he was.

"Pass up the purse and the camera bag. Now!"

Tera slid the strap over her head and handed purse to Gray Hair, who tossed it to the passenger side floor. Gary handed his camera bag over and gave a wince when the same was done to it.

"You'll find seat belts back there," their abductor said. "Get 'em on."

As the Wraithworths complied, he backed the Ford out of the fire department lot onto Scenic Heights. Gray Hair held the gun on them, manipulating the gear shift and steering wheel with one skillful hand. Once in drive, pointed the car eastward and accelerated casually.

"There are handcuffs back there on the floor," Gray Hair said as he drove. The barrel of the gun was no longer on them but pointed at the roof. His eyes, hidden by aviator sunglasses, seemed to watch them in the rearview mirror. "Gary, pick them up. Hand one pair to the missus and put the other on yourself. And no funny shit. I want to hear the clicks. Hold up your hands and let me see."

Gary sighed and, looking to Tera, who was silently crying, reluctantly snapped on the cuffs. She followed suit and sobbed.

***

The sound of a police car's siren took Firefighter Tim Stehr's eyes from the truck window he was cleaning. Just outside the station, a white unmarked cruiser stopped in front of two pedestrians.

From inside the fire engine, he could hear none of the conversation, but it was plain that the man and woman they had stopped did not look happy about it.

Stehr slid from the driver's seat, dropped to the freshly mopped cement floor, and took a few steps toward the open garage door. He squinted but was unable to see anything through the window tint.

"Hey, Stosh," he called to his fellow fireman. "Look at this."

Stosh, a much shorter, dark curly-haired man, dropped his wet sponge into the bucket and stood up from the wheel he was washing.

"What?"

"What do you think is happenin' here?" Tim asked.

Stosh rolled his eyes. "Oh, come on. Not this game again."

"No, really. Look," Stehr repeated and pointed to the white sedan.

Stosh looked. His lips curled from boredom at first, but as he watched the two people get into the back of the car, his mouth straightened. "Hmmph."

"Since when does EPPD allow window tint?" Stehr posed.

"Could be a detective from the county...or the state," Stosh said. "They can buy their own—hey. What's he doin'?"

The two firemen watched as the expressions of both people turned from discomfort to terror. Then, the woman got into the back seat, followed by the man.

"They don't look like they want to go for that ride," Stehr opined.

"They sure don't," Stosh agreed as the car backed up into the road. "I don't think that's a cop."

Something was not right, and both men knew it. Tim jogged into the sunlight and focused his eyes on the license plate. He read it out loud several times and pulled out his cellphone. Opening the memo app, he typed it in and saved it.

Tim turned to Stosh, who had joined him. "I think I should call the cops, don't you?"

"Sure," Stosh agreed. "Should we mention *that*, too?" he asked and pointed.

Tim looked in time to see a black, older model Chevy SUV angle into the driveway and pull a U-turn. The tires squealed from the stress of the tight turn and the engine bleated loudly through dual exhaust pipes when the driver accelerated after the white Ford.

"Iowa plates," Tim murmured. "Shit. Didn't catch the number."

"Yeah, maybe call the cops, Tim," Stosh said. "Somethin's not right with that."

***

Del turned onto Mitchell Road, northbound and drove in silence, grinning over the fact that the Wraithworths were too terrified to speak.

He had not driven very long when he spotted a black truck in his mirror. The truck was tall and changed lanes whenever he did.

Hampton needed to contact Anderson anyway, so when he saw an opportunity to turn off Mitchell, he took it.

He flipped on the strobing red and blue lights and moved to the right lane, just before the next intersection. The cars on his right slowed down and pulled to the shoulder. He noted the black SUV in his mirrors as it continued north on Mitchell. He hung the first left into the parking lot of an ornate white building that looked more like a mansion than a commercial site. When he saw the establishment's sign by the road, he laughed and laughed hard.

"What's funny?" Gary called from the back seat. "Why are we at a funeral home?"

"Shut up!" Hampton burs and parked the car in the shade of a tree.

"Tell us what you want," Gary tried again.

"I want you—" Del began and brought the 1911 up for his passengers to see, "—to shut your Goddamn mouth!" He watched Gary's reaction in the rearview mirror and smirked.

Gary did as he was told and reached for his wife's cuffed hands. She was too frightened to talk. Her bottom lip quivered, and tears dropped from her reddened face. Seeing this sparked anger in Gary. He gave the door handle a tug, but it was locked.

"Hey! Knock that off," Gray Hair warned.

"What...did you engage the childproof locks on this piece of shit?" he challenged. "This is no cop car, bud, and you're no cop!"

Del spun around and swung the big handgun. Gary was quick to keep it from striking his face. The barrel of the pistol impacted his right forearm, hard.

151

Gary shouted in pain and cursed loudly. Tera let out a scream.

"Shut the fuck up and stay still!" Gray Hair exploded over their noise. He aimed for Gary's face and held the gun there for many long seconds. "I'll make you hurt, Wraithworth. Don't push me."

"All right," Gary answered with his palms up. "All right."

Their captor turned from them, picked up a cellphone, and made a call.

"Hey, it's me," he said. "I have them. Yeah." He turned in the driver's seat and watched his prisoners. "Have you heard from the boss?"

Gary looked out the darkened window, seeing the traffic on Mitchell Road buzz along. He hoped that a cop would drive by and notice them, but he supposed there was nothing unusual about a car sitting in a parking lot.

Gray Hair's attention was focused on a tablet or perhaps a laptop the Wraithworths could not see. The bench seat blocked their view, but the glow of the screen reflected in Gray Hair's sunglasses. He grunted and mumbled in the positive or the negative as he listened to the person on the other end of his cellphone call.

Tera nudged her husband, who turned to her and found that she had pulled her phone out of her pants pocket. While there was still no service, her finger was set next to a circle on the display labeled, 'Emergency Call.' Gary knew that a cellular phone with no network could still be used to call 9-1-1. He looked into her reddened eyes and gave a tiny nod.

Tera pressed the circle and 'Calling 9-1-1 Emergency' appeared on the display. Gary smiled briefly, then looked to their abductor, who was still focused on the screen of whatever it was that he was using.

"Yeah, that looks like a good spot," Gray Hair said.

Good spot? Holy crap! Good spot for what? Gary wondered. His heart stopped when a tiny voice emanated from Tera's phone.

"*Nine-one-one. What is your emergency?*" a female operator asked.

"Hey!" Gray Hair tossed his cellphone onto the dash and swung the 1911 into Tera's face. "Hand it over or you're a stain," he growled.

Tera lifted her phone up to him and squeezed her eyes shut.

"*Hello? Are you there?*" the 9-1-1 operator asked.

Gray Hair snatched the phone from her hand and ended the call. Into his own, he spoke. "Call you back in a minute." He dropped his cell to the seat and shoved the gun into Gary's face. "Where's yours?"

"In the camera bag," he answered. "Side pocket."

Without taking his gun or his eyes from the Wraithworths, their tormentor sat with his back against the steering wheel and reached for the bag. He unzipped the pocket and fished out the phone.

"All right," he said through clenched teeth, "you don't move. If I see movement back here, you're both dead." His eyes were still a mystery behind the aviators, but his intensity was evident in his words.

Their captor looked about the parking lot and stashed the pistol into his shoulder holster. He opened the driver's door, and as they watched, Gray Hair dropped Tera's phone to the pavement and began stomping it with the heel of his brown, western-style boots. The phone quickly broke down into hundreds of shards of plastic and metal.

"Gare," Tera said in a shaky voice. "If I never get another chance to tell you. I love you."

Gary took her cuffed hands in his. "I love you, too. We'll get out of this."

As he spoke these words, movement behind Gray Hair caught his eye. An older SUV, black and raised on off-road tires, left its parking space on the street and pulled into the parking lot.

Gary's heart sank. Gray Hair had help.

As he watched the approaching truck, he gripped his wife's hands. She noticed him looking behind her and she turned.

The sound of the approaching vehicle caused their captor to look over his shoulder. It quickly became evident that he had no idea who was in the black truck. Gray Hair stopped his maniacal destruction and backed toward the open car door. He reached for his weapon, and when he did, the driver of the truck accelerated.

"Oh…shiiiit," Tera let out on an exhale.

Gary pulled her toward him and covered her head. She buried her face in his chest, repeating her mantra of profanity.

Gray Hair moved behind his car door and aimed his gun at the truck's windshield. The SUV driver hit his brakes hard. The momentum bled away quickly in a mass of tire smoke, but enough remained for the SUV to hit the Crown Vic's door. Gray Hair became pinned at the chest in between the door and the roof of the car. His right arm was pinched at the wrist, leaving the 1911's barrel pointed toward the sky.

Gray Hair let out a howl of pain mixed with rage. He began cussing in a strangled voice at the truck's driver.

Gary saw a figure cross in front of the Crown Vic. It was a short, stout man, wearing a dark blue suit, a narrow-brimmed black fedora, and wayfarer sunglasses.

"Help! Back here!" Gary called.

Their roundish rescuer tried to open both doors on the passenger side, but they were locked. From his jacket pocket, he withdrew a small baton, extended it to at least twice its length, and shattered the front door's window.

"You guys get ready to get in that truck!" he shouted as he reached for the power lock switch.

Gary and Tera needed not be told twice. They released their seatbelts over the gargled threats of Gray Hair. The driver of the SUV yanked the rear door open and Gary jumped out, turning to help his wife out of the car.

"Come on!" the stout man shouted. He was already a few steps away from them, heading back to the open driver's door of his truck.

"Go! Go!" Gary shouted at Tera. She sprinted around the back of the Ford on her way to the mystery rescuer's vehicle.

Gary risked retrieving his camera bag and his wife's purse. He pulled the front door out of his way and grabbed them both by the straps, then his eyes locked on a familiar object. It was his own laptop. Gray Hair had taken it from their house and had been trying to guess the password.

"Hey! Come on!" their rescuer shouted and hopped into his truck.

Gary snatched the computer from the seat, shook off the broken glass, and followed his wife's path. Clumsily, he opened the passenger side rear door and dove in. Immediately, the SUV was thrust backward, dumping Gary onto the floor in a jumble of limbs. The brakes were hit hard, throwing the door shut. The truck surged forward in a shriek of tires.

He heard a shot and then another, followed by a metallic clank.

All Gary could see was carpet. All Tera could see was dashboard and sky. She was in the front seat and holding onto the interior of the SUV for dear life.

"Stay down!" their new friend shouted unnecessarily.

The SUV bounded over the funeral home's lawn, down a curb and, through a volley of car horns and tire squeals, hopped onto Mitchell Road and headed south with all eight cylinders singing.

Gary grabbed the back of the seat in one handcuffed fist and righted himself. His heart pounded as he looked through the windows for the white Ford.

Their rescuer was quickly putting cars behind them and, as Mitchell Road curved to the southwest, there continued to be no sign of Gray Hair.

"Is everybody all right?" the driver called over the din of the motor. He let off the gas as he came up on traffic.

Gary heard his wife answer in the affirmative. She was as out of breath as he was.

"Mr. Wraithworth?" The driver caught his eyes in the rearview mirror.

"Yeah." Gary nodded. "Okay."

"Good," the driver said. "I'm Dennis, by the way. Dennis Archen." He braked the truck hard at the intersection beyond the overpass and turned onto Highway 212, eastbound. "By the way, I sure hope whatever it was you took from his car was important. It coulda gotcha killed!"

"It was." Gary leaned forward to see where they were headed. He noticed his wife look at him quizzically. He held up the laptop.

"Holy shit," she whispered. "He was in our *house.*"

"All right, well, whatever," dismissed Dennis as he accelerated and changed lanes. His eyes darted from mirror to mirror. "We ditched him. With any luck, I broke some bones."

"How…just how−?" started Gary.

"I'll explain," Dennis took up and waved him off. "I'm a private investigator. I've been following the doings of your friend for a while."

"Who is he? What is he?" Gary nearly shouted.

"I don't know how much Greely told you, but his name's Del Hampton. He's FBI, but he's gone dark. He's on the Bureau's payroll, but he really works for a group of billionaires. Political assassination, abductions, bombings, whatever they want."

"You mean The Council?"

"That's them. My colleagues and I are still investigating the organization," Dennis explained as he drove. "We're pretty sure we only have a partial list of members."

"So, you know David?" Tera asked.

"Yeah, he's been working with us," Archen confirmed. "It was my idea that he reach out to fellow websleuths to gain attention to Hampton and his handlers."

"Looks like it worked," Gary said sardonically.

"What we do know is that the members of The Council are all extreme right-wing," Archen continued. "Most of them are Old Money."

"So…we're talking conspiracy theory-type stuff?" Gary asked.

"It's no theory, Mr. Wraithworth," Dennis answered. "You've seen those videos. You've featured them on your channel."

"But you have proof of an FBI connection?"

"I have a partial papertrail, you might say. And there's emails. There used to be a liaison in the FBI, but he was eliminated a long time ago. Hampton is an active agent, but his doings are not sanctioned by the Bureau. Because of his connections to the men with deep pockets, no one's asked about him."

"Is that how he gets to impersonate police officers?" Tera interjected.

"It helps," Dennis said with an emphatic nod. "He gets away with murder–literally–and covers it up with help from his employers."

The wayfarer sunglasses obscured the man's eyes, but Gary could see Dennis glance at him in the mirror.

"Where are you taking us?" Tera asked.

"We're going to my place," Archen replied. "It's not safe for you at home. Obviously."

"Why not just take us to the police?" Gary questioned.

"I'm not sure *that's* safe either," Dennis said and tossed his hands up in the air. "Even I don't know just how far The Council can reach."

"Mr. Archen–" Tera began.

"Just call me Dennis, Mrs. Wraithworth," he said and smiled.

"Only if you call me Tera."

"Sure thing, Tera."

"Do you have any idea how we can ditch these?" she asked him and rattled her cuffs.

"Oh! Sure," Dennis blurted and palmed his forehead, sending the short-brimmed fedora askew. "In the back is a big black box. Behind you, Mr. Wraithworth."

"You can call me Gary."

"It's really nice to meet you both," Archen said. "Anyway, if you open the box, and pull out the top tray, there's a compartment underneath. I have a whole bunch of handcuff keys."

Gary bent over the back of the seat and found the box. It was heavy and thick plastic. He turned it toward himself and unlatched it. Beneath the top tray were a lot of different types of keys on rings, but after fishing about for a moment, he retrieved what he thought looked like a ring of handcuff keys. He tried half them before finding the one that worked. Once free, he unlocked Tera.

"I don't even know what to say, Dennis," Gary said, leaning forward and looking to their rescuer.

"Thank you, at the very least," Tera added.

"Forget about it," Dennis waved off. "Hampton made a rare mistake and left himself vulnerable. I'm just glad it worked."

"Well, you risked getting shot, so it's a big deal to us," Gary assured him and patted the man's shoulder.

Archen smiled. "I had to, folks. Del Hampton's gotten away with murder far too long."

***

Del's world turned dark from the lack of oxygen, and for several long seconds, all he could sense was the heat from the truck's engine, the pain in his chest, shoulders, and right wrist.

He was dimly aware that his captives were being released, and then, just as suddenly as it had occurred, the pressure applied to his body was gone. Instinctively, he began pumping air in and out of his lungs in a mad pace.

The next thing he knew, he fell back onto the driver's seat and his sight returned to him. The sound of the truck's roaring motor prompted him to shake away the fuzz. Instead of coming back to hit him a second time, he watched the SUV driving away.

To a seasoned killer like Del Hampton, this gesture of mercy was stupid. He pulled himself out of the car and, still dizzy, he brought his heavy and sore right arm up to aim his pistol at the fleeing truck. The effort to squeeze off a shot was more than his body was ready for.

The first shot pulled left and low, sending the bullet into the grass. He held his right wrist with his left and tried again.

The second shot struck the bumper.

As the SUV bounded onto the road, Hampton tried to focus on the license plate. He thought about pursuing but was aware of pain in his ribs and right forearm.

Del returned his 1911 to the holster and sat back down. A bolt of pain shot through his midsection and, pressing the tips of two fingers along his ribs, he quickly found the sore spot. He was sure that one, perhaps two were bruised.

He picked up his cellphone and called Anderson. "Hey. We have a problem. I have a vehicle description and a partial plate."

Chapter Twelve

*D*ennis Archen's place was in the next town of Edina, so their drive was short. The Wraithworths were familiar with the neighboring town, but not the upscale neighborhood.

The winding road was shadowed by trees, giving the recently-freed couple a sense of warmth and security.

Dennis slowed for a left turn and Gary read the street sign for Indian Hill Circle. The road curved tightly to the right and the SUV swung into the first driveway on the left.

"What a lovely home," Tera marveled.

"Thanks," Archen replied and stopped the truck. "Sit tight a minute. Don't get out yet."

"Okay," she answered and looked back at her husband.

Gary shrugged, and watched Archen jog to the attached garage's side door. He disappeared inside, and the garage door opened. He quickly walked back to the SUV and drove it inside.

"Okay, folks," he said as he cut the motor, "we're all clear."

Tera hopped out, meeting Gary on her side. She drew him close and they embraced tightly.

Dennis pulled open the tailgate and retrieved a suitcase. Then another, followed by his black plastic box. He squeezed past the couple, pressed the button to close the overhead door, and went inside.

Gary whispered, "Let me help him with his things."

"'Kay," she replied and let him go.

Wraithworth bent to pick up the black box and grunted. "Holy…crap," he wheezed and walked inside.

"Holy crap is right," Tera said as she took in the huge kitchen on their left. A high-ceilinged living room swept along to the right. The rooms were lit by the unrestricted sunlight pouring through the windows.

"Oh, hey, thank you, Gary," Dennis said, noting what he had brought inside. "That's a heavy sucker."

Gary nodded, stunned by just how short Archen was now that they were facing each other. He doubted that Archen was even five-feet tall.

"Be right back," Dennis said and went back into the garage. He closed the SUV's tailgate returned to find the Wraithworths standing in the middle of the living room, just taking in the décor. "Hey, you two. It might not be safe to be standing in the window."

Gary nodded and quickly found the strings for the curtains and drapes. The room darkened as he closed them.

"I guess he could have tailed us," Tera said and shrugged. She found a light switch and lit the room.

"We can't dismiss the possibility, Tera. I'm sorry," Dennis offered and removed his shades, revealing his soulful brown eyes. He smiled with regret. "Del Hampton can't be underestimated. *Ever*."

"What's our next move then?" Gary asked.

"Just make yourselves at home," Dennis said and removed his hat. His black hair was cut short and the hairline was receding. "I need some time to think."

"We all do after today," Tera added and sat down on the thickly padded, brown leather couch.

Archen showed them where the coffee maker was and excused himself to take a shower. He disappeared down the hallway that began on the other end of the living room and they heard him walk up an uncarpeted staircase.

"Nice place," Tera commented as she wandered casually into the kitchen.

"Yep," Gary answered absently. He took another look around at the lavishly decorated room as he sat back into the couch.

The television was giant to their standards, a sixty-inch screen set above a marble fireplace. He found the remote control on the coffee table and turned it on. He searched around a bit, switching from one national news channel to the next. He found no further coverage of David Greely's death.

Tera sauntered back into the room, two cups of coffee in her hands. She set one on the table in front of Gary. "Should we check the local channels in case there's news about us?"

"I doubt there would be, but I'll check," he replied and found a Minneapolis morning show. The hosts were focused on the solar eclipse, supposedly to happen later that day. Gary left it on with the volume low.

"Well, he reads," Tera said and picked up a hardback book from a short stack on the end table. "I don't see our hero reading chick lit, though, Gare," she said and held it out for her husband to see.

Gary smiled. "Well, maybe he has a wife or a daughter."

He wandered about the large room, checking out the family photographs on the walls. There was not one that featured Dennis Archen. The male in most of them bore no resemblance to Archen, and the woman was almost certainly that man's wife. Two small children, a boy and a girl, posed with the adults in most of the pictures.

Gary ventured into the hall. He encountered a large bathroom, complete with an oversized tub and a double sink. The walls were clad in an ornate dark wood and, giving it a knock, it sounded sturdy, not just a particle board paneling.

He reentered the hallway and found that Tera had followed him. Across from the bathroom was a sitting room with a bookcase stuffed to overfilling. Two comfortable-looking chairs and a chaise were set on a plush beige carpet. A furnished patio stood outside beyond sliding glass doors.

"Love it," Tera said quietly.

Gary agreed and stepped toward the spiraling wooden staircase. He passed a spotless guest bedroom along the way. At the foot of the stairs, he stopped and remained perfectly still, listening.

"He's showering all right," Tera whispered from behind him.

Gary ran his hands through his hair. It was greasy from the sweat he had accumulated. While he thought things through, he continued checking out the place, stepping to the end of the hall.

"Whoa," he murmured.

The hall emptied into a high-ceilinged room with three of its four walls made of glass panels. There were several matching black leather couches and chairs, either lining the walls or encircling coffee tables. At their far left was a grand piano, set upon a raised platform. To their right was an immense bar with padded leather stools.

The room was surrounded, in effect, by nature, as the lake could be seen beyond the piano and the trees bordered the other walls. Two skylights, embedded deeply into the ceiling and bracketed by elegant wooden beams, directed the sunlight throughout.

"Holy crap," Tera proclaimed. She stepped further inside and turned around. Looking up, she saw that the second floor terminated into a balcony, looking down upon the entire room.

Frowning, Gary left the ballroom and bounded up the stairs. His athletic shoes squeaked on the polished wood.

"Gare?" Tera called after him. As he disappeared into the upstairs hallway, she went after him.

Gary followed the sound of the shower to the open door at the end of the hallway, passing two large bedrooms and a bathroom on the left and a home theater room and a den on his right.

As he entered the room at the end, the water stopped. It was the master bedroom and had its own full bath.

"Dennis?" he called. The sound of a sliding shower door and movement came from behind the closed door. "I think we need to talk."

"What's wrong?" Archen called from within. He sounded out of breath, as if he were drying himself quickly. "He didn't find us, did he?"

"Just come out when you can, please."

"Gare. What the hell?" Tera whispered from his side.

"This isn't his house."

"Don't you think you're being just a tad critical of a guy that got us away from that maniac?" she asked quietly, though her eyes said she was short of furious.

"The book, Tera, belongs to the girl in the family photos on the wall," Gary explained and gestured to the bathroom door. "And *this* guy isn't in *any* of 'em."

Tera sighed with disappointment and crossed her arms. "Just don't go off on him." She shook her long brown hair from her face and flashed her pale blue eyes thoughtfully.

Dennis yanked the bathroom door out of his way and stepped into the bedroom. He was still damp and wore only a giant white bath towel around his waist. Gary took a step back, as did Tera as she swung her eyes to admire the balcony doors on the other side of the room.

"Okay, what−?" Archen gasped and hopped back behind the door. "Jesus! What the hell is it with you two?"

"Er−sorry, Dennis," Gary fumbled and looked to Tera, who was now inspecting the skylight. "Look, um…somethin's just not right here. This isn't really your house, is it?"

"That question couldn't have waited a few minutes? I'm still dripping wet," Dennis protested. His eyebrows darted high into his forehead and he appeared hurt, but amused.

"After all we've been through today…I don't know, Dennis," Gary said and spread his arms wide. "Nothing seems right. We're scared and not entirely trusting."

Archen sighed heavily. "I'm dog sitting," he offered, though his shifting eyes and dancing eyebrows said otherwise.

Gary spread his arms with the palms out and he pretended to search the carpet for the animal. "Dog? There's no dog!"

"Okay, okay. Give me a minute," their rescuer surrendered and shut the door.

Gary looked to Tera and both shook their heads as if they were one mind. They walked back into the hallway and pondered the framed prints hung on the light coffee-colored walls as they waited.

In a few moments, Archen emerged from the master bedroom, dressed in fresh clothes. He had ditched the blue suit for a black one. The Wraithworths said nothing as they watched him approach, suit jacket in hand.

"Okay, so, you're right," the shorter man said to them. "This isn't my place, as I may have led you to believe."

"*May* have?" Tera interjected. "You said the words, 'my place.'"

"Yeah, I know. Sorry," Archen said. "Look. This is a client's home and I've been invited to use it when I need to. They're out of the country until next week. In any other circumstances, I would've hid you guys out at some cheap motel, but this was an emergency. I needed to get all of us and my truck out of sight."

"And if—what did you say his name was?" Gary took up.

"Del Hampton," Dennis filled in.

Gary repeated the name to help remember it. "If he had tracked us here, what then?"

"I think at that point, criminal trespass charges would be the least of your problems. Correct me if I'm wrong," Archen said. "Let me explain this once and for all…downstairs. I need coffee."

In the kitchen, Archen stood watching the coffee machine fill the mug while Gary and Tera waited, seated upon the breakfast bar stools.

"So, I have to tell you I'm thinking of writing a book on this Hampton guy and his relationship with The Council."

"Aren't we all?" Gary commented dryly.

With a crooked grin, Archen continued. He stood on the other side of the counter from them and began adding creamer to the mug. "Like I mentioned, members of The Council are made up of some Old Money families. Industrialists dating back to the late eighteen-hundreds. There's a minority sub-group in there that are *nouveau riche*." He paused for a sip. "You know, New Money," he added with his fingers making air quotes.

"We know," Tera said. "Go on."

Dennis rolled his eyes playfully. "Anyway, as you can imagine, they're very involved politically. A lot of them have been pulling the economic strings of not only the U.S., but the world."

"So, they hired a cleaner of sorts?" asked Gary.

"Exactly," Dennis agreed. "There's nothing really new about it, though. A lot of crimes have been perpetrated on behalf of the rich throughout the world. It's a timeless activity of the elite."

"What makes this Hampton guy so special?" Tera asked.

"Not a thing," Dennis said plainly. "The only reason we even know about him is that there are cameras everywhere."

"That's been bugging me, Dennis," Gary interjected. "Why are there so few recordings of this guy?"

"There's probably a ton more that have been erased," he explained. "A lot of what has surfaced was kept back from being destroyed by people paid to do so. Charlie Durand, for instance. He was to get rid of the footage of Hampton driving that borrowed Louisiana State Trooper car. Charlie was thinking of using it as blackmail, felt guilty about it, then sent it to us through Greely."

"Is that how this started? With that video?" Gary asked.

Dennis took a drink before answering. "We had some other evidence, but after that one, all the other stuff came out of the woodwork. The killings of Durand and Greely will probably scare anyone else from coming forward," Archen explained.

"You think Hampton's been around awhile?" Tera asked.

"We think he's been working for The Council since the '80s. There weren't so many cameras in public way back then and, as you can imagine. Anything they did grab was pretty low resolution."

Gary nodded, understanding Dennis's point. Low quality cameras and film made it hard to identify people with certainty.

"Hampton is ex-Green Beret," said Archen. "He carried out a lot of CIA-sponsored missions in South America. You know, the 'war on drugs' farce. He became a fed after that and went on a lot of undercover jobs. Eventually, he went dark and worked The Council."

"So, someone on this Council must be a high-ranking official in the FBI," Gary supposed.

"He'd have to be to hide the money trail and keep Hampton's missions off the books," Dennis agreed.

"What were you and Greely trying to accomplish?" Tera asked.

"We want to expose him *and* The Council," Dennis answered as if it was obvious.

Gary and Tera shared a look of doubt but said nothing.

Archen noticed the glance. "Hey, look, I know how it sounds," he conceded, "but someone had to take a stand. This kind of crazy shit is what conspiracy nuts have been talkin' about for ages. Who knew they were a little bit right?"

Gary agreed. He had covered plenty of such stories on his channel.

"Anyway, YouTuber guys like Greely, a few private investigators like myself, former FBI, and other retired law enforcement, started putting their knowledge together late last year. Soon, we had enough to start a file on this stuff."

"That tells me there are a lot of people on the inside in almost every case," said Gary.

Dennis nodded. "Money buys a lot of silence. I guess, though, some people have a good conscience."

"Where are you really from, Dennis?" Gary asked as he sauntered to the counter for more coffee.

"St. Louis," he replied. "Me and Greely met at a writer's convention and discovered we didn't live too far apart. I wrote a couple of crime novels and he found 'em interesting. Anyway, he hung around a bit and then he mentioned Bill Welks. I told him that Welks and I used to be pals, so we got to talking about his disappearance. Anyway, that's how this whole thing snowballed."

"You knew Welks?" asked Gary.

"I did. He was a good man. A bit too politically opinionated and that's what got him the wrong kind of attention."

"Do you think he's dead?"

Dennis responded with a nod as his eyebrows arched in regret. He sat back and sighed. "He wrote a good number of books about politics and I'm torn between which one got 'im killed."

"I'm guessing it was the one about the senator and his mistress," Tera opined. "That killed that man's run for President and broke up his marriage."

"There's where you're wrong, young lady," said Dennis as he leaned forward and rested his chin on his hands. "That senator has no connection to The Council. I'd bet the farm on the neo-Nazi novel. It was branded as fiction but loosely based on a true story. Welks even said so publicly."

"Then the men paying Hampton's tab are white supremacists," Gary concluded.

"That's exactly what they are," Archen agreed. "There are some Klan members mixed in there, too."

"But what the hell are we supposed to do about *any* of this?" Tera blurted in a tone of exasperation.

Dennis gave a smile to her then turned to Gary. "Is your camera still in that bag?"

__Chapter Thirteen__

*H*ampton sat still behind the wheel of the Crown Vic, cradling his gun hand. The wrist had been pinched badly in the doorframe, and the bruises were already forming. He flexed it to make sure nothing was broken. Pain flared when he did, but his range of motion was intact.

He kept his eyes moving over the landscape and his mirrors. He had fired twice at the fleeing SUV, and so far, the only reaction had been a resident of a home across the street who opened her front door and peered out. She seemed not to see him beyond the glare of the windshield when her elderly eyes set upon the car. After a moment, she gave up and closed it again.

On the chance that someone had called the authorities, Del started the car and casually pulled out onto the side street, turning east, away from Mitchell Road.

His eye caught the flickering glimmer at his left. The driver's side mirror vibrated as he drove. The housing was cracked and looked as if it would fall off any moment.

As the seconds passed, the rage within him built. In his mind, he saw himself torturing the Wraithworths to death. He would start with the woman and make the husband watch. His bit his lip as he thought of the slow torture, cutting her extremities, her torso, her breasts, and so on. He would bleed her, break her, make her cry for mercy, and finally, when he was satisfied that her husband was mentally disassembled by the view, he would dismember her, just for the fun.

Then, he would turn his attentions on Gary, though it would certainly be less satisfying without an audience. For Del, there was no sexual gratification in these acts. The pleasure he derived was based solely on the power and control he held over his victims. He liked to inflict pain and hold the fate of a helpless human being in his hands.

He took great pleasure in building up the hope in an individual, the hope that he may stop his torture and set his victim free. He relished in dashing that hope to pieces when the torture resumed. He loved to hear the begging and the screams.

Glory and blood. Glory and blood.

Del took a deep breath, let out a great whoop of joy, and shook the happy images away. He needed to focus on his next task, which was to change cars. He had been seen by his victims and possibly others after taking shots at the truck.

He took several turns through the residential neighborhood, watching his mirrors for police vehicles. Driving on Mitchell Road once again, he found a strip mall with a large parking lot and headed for it. In little time, he saw a prime target and parked nose-to-nose. It was a Nissan Altima, an exceedingly common vehicle. It was the color of sand, also low profile.

Hampton kept an eye on his surroundings as he fished through his car thief's kit. He placed a squat dish-shaped antenna on his dashboard, aimed it directly at the Nissan, and attached its USB cord to the laptop. He waited for the Altima's computer to search for its owner's key fob with a radio signal.

Del smiled when the computer locked onto the manufacturer's code. He typed it into the computer, plugged the programmable key fob into another port and waited some more.

He looked around and saw no one walking about. A car rolled by behind him, its driver looking for a parking space.

When the software indicated that it was finished programming, Del held the fob up and pressed the button that would unlock the Nissan's doors and disarm the alarm. When he heard a light beep and saw the car's lights flash, he knew he was in business.

Del returned the antenna and laptop back into his briefcase, then popped the trunks of both cars.

Getting out of the Ford, he casually looked around, his eyes shielded by his sunglasses. A few people were walking through the parking lot, along with a couple cars cruising through the rows. He shut the door and turned in time to see the Ford's mirror drop to the blacktop in a clatter of plastic and glass. Hampton sighed.

He walked up to the passenger side of the Altima and opened the door. He deposited his briefcase and strode to the Ford's trunk. He dumped the broken mirror inside and picked up his large suitcase. He stood there for a moment, typing a text for Kenny Anderson. He gave the location of the Crown Victoria and orders for it to be retrieved by an operative, usually a low-level employee of the FBI. A car porter of sorts. They would pick it up and either dispose of it or return it to the pool.

Hampton saw no one in the cars near him and no pedestrians in his aisle. Quickly, he reached down and snatched the phony plate that had been magnetized over the real one and slid it under his sport coat. Del transferred his case to the Nissan's trunk, quickly slid behind the wheel, and pressed the button to start the engine. With the freshly programmed fob in his jacket pocket, the car's computer was easily fooled. The engine started, and in a moment, Del Hampton was out of the parking lot, driving casually in the direction the black SUV had gone.

He picked his phone from his pocket and called Anderson. "Hey," he said when Kenny answered. "I had to switch cars."

"What happened?"

Del Hampton relayed the story and his eyes settled on his bruised wrist. The aching area of purple infuriated him.

"Damn. Do you need me to arrange back-up?" Kenny asked.

"No. I want to take care of these people myself. Do me a favor. I need you to go through Bureau channels and send out an APB."

"Sure thing," Kenny said and shifted in his chair to type. "Go ahead."

"Black full-size GM SUV. Mid-to-late nineties model. First three letters of the plate are Charlie, Mike, Victor."

"Got it. Last seen?"

"Heading north on Mitchell Road, Eden Prairie. I want the description of the Wraithworths issued, along with the driver. Little guy on the stout side. Dark blue suit and black hat. List them all armed and dangerous. That'll get the attention."

"Okay. Anything else, Del?"

"Just tell the boss I'm on it and that we're just delayed. Objective is still in play."

***

Kenny Anderson sat back in his comfortably-worn office chair and scratched his nose in thought. He had felt for a long time that Hampton was allowing himself to become obsessed with the Wraithworths. Long road trips were commonplace in their line of work, but Del was more interested in taking the car than flying to Minneapolis. In doing so, it was likely he had lost any advantage of surprise. He could have easily disposed of them while they slept had he flown. Instead, they were on the loose.

Anderson sighed heavily and picked up the telephone wired to one of his computers. He typed the number on his keyboard and made the call via the internet, using an encrypted connection. He waited through four rings and then heard a click. The call had been answered.

"Hello, Mr. H," Kenny began and swallowed hard. "I think we have a problem."

"Do go on," replied the southern-accented voice, fortified by time into a sandy-finished smoothness.

"I'm sorry to say, sir, but I believe we have a problem with D."

"I see. I've been afraid of that," Edwin Holloway said.

The Holloway family owned or were partners of several fast food and soft drink corporations. Edwin Holloway was one of the many great-grandsons of the business's founder and a permanent liaison between the field operatives and The Council.

"Oh?" Kenny Anderson replied. Holloway had never expressed concern about Hampton.

"A number of issues have come to the public eye," Edwin explained. "He has been with us for many years. Perhaps too long."

"He's taking too many chances, in my opinion, sir. He is closing on our targets, but they're giving him some trouble. I asked if he wanted back-up, but he refused."

"So, he has allowed it to become personal," Edwin Holloway concluded.

"Beyond personal, sir."

"I understand." Holloway was silent for a moment, perhaps to take a drink, then sighed. "Well, I will confer with colleagues and get back to you. In the meantime, get a pair of reliable men. Prepare flights to Minneapolis for them. At the very least, we may need to reel D in."

"I'm on it."

***

In a second-floor bedroom, Gary sat behind the wooden desk, going over his handwritten script once more. His camera was in Tera's hands, as the tripod had been left at home. Gary took a deep breath and Tera gave him a thumb up. Dennis stood next to her and slightly behind, watching Gary's face intently.

"Hello, *Wraithworks* fans," Gary began and cleared his throat. "As you've probably noticed, the *Wraithworks* channel has been shut down. I can't get any information about how or why it was done, but a few of our fellow YouTubers have had their channels deleted as well. We all had something in common. We followed and featured a series of videos by the creator of *RydingtheRails,* featuring the Killer Agent videos. That channel has also been removed, but I'm here to tell you that this is a very real agent." Gary swallowed hard, thinking of David Greely.

"This man came to our house this morning. My wife and I tried to get to the police station, but he found us and forced us into his car. If it wasn't for the heroic deed by a...well, I guess I should say a bystander, we'd probably be dead right now." Gary halted a moment and looked to Dennis and Tera for approval. Both nodded and Tera gestured for him to continue.

"Look, guys, we need your help. We're in hiding and safe for the moment, thanks to our rescuer, but we need all the shares of this that we can. This Killer Agent, whose name we do now know to be Del Hampton, a renegade FBI agent, is after us and has connections with law enforcement. We have no idea what he could be telling police about us, so we can't call them for help."

Gary halted once again and looked at Tera. He gestured for her to join him, for the first time ever, in front of the camera. She shook her head, but he insisted. She sighed and handed the camera to Dennis, who took it in hand and held it as she had.

"Ladies and gentlemen," Gary said as Tera moved closely to him, "this is Tera, my wife. She and I have run the *Wraithworks* channel for a few years now and it's been our life. All we can say now is that because of it, we and other YouTubers have uncovered a deep conspiracy and it must be stopped."

Wraithworth gave a detailed description of Del Hampton and the car that they had escaped from. With a final plea for viewers and fellow YouTubers to share the story, Gary signed off.

"Okay, so now what?" Tera asked.

Dennis handed the camera back to her. "The way I figure it, you two need to work your editing magic and put it on a thumb drive. From there, I can get it somewhere with wi-fi so I can upload it to your file sharing site. I don't want you using the wi-fi here. We can't chance it."

Gary said, "I think making an alternate YouTube channel would be good, too. We can get on Twitter and spread the word there."

"We can put it on the website," Tera interjected. "Then we should email the link to Daisy."

"Her channel's shut down, too, but she can forward it to others," Gary said.

Tera nodded.

"All that may be aiming a little high," Archen inserted. "I can find the library a few towns over and use their computer. While I'm at it, how about I send it to the media? Newspaper, local TV," he said and shrugged, hinting for opinions.

Gary shrugged with him. "Can't hurt to try."

"I agree," Tera said. "But couldn't Hampton have reported you to the police, Dennis? If he's still in good with the Bureau–"

"Well, sure as shit, you two can't go," Dennis asserted and pointed a stubby finger at one, then the other. "You two need to sit tight. Besides, if he got my license plate, it won't help him."

"Oh, boy," Gary groaned. "And why is that, Dennis?"

"I borrowed it."

"Come *on!*" Gary begged in exasperation.

"What? I was going to put it back in a couple days."

"Dennis—" Tera folded her arms and cocked her hip, eyeing him suspiciously.

"It's no problem. Nothing to worry about. I have another plate I can use," Dennis said.

"*Another* plate? Another *borrowed* plate?" Gary said in a raised voice.

"Hey! Enough already!" Dennis shouted, ending the protests. He immediately softened and sighed. "Look, I'm no rookie. I know what I'm doing. Just get this vid edited, *tout suite*. 'Kay?"

The Wraithworths remained unmoved. They glanced at each other, unsure.

"Come on!" Archen urged. "*Chop-chop!*"

They shrugged in unison, and Gary sat at the desk and opened his laptop.

Dennis left the room, headed into the garage, and went around to the back of his truck. He rummaged about the compartment where the spare tire tools were kept, retrieved a Minnesota license plate and a screwdriver. In minutes, he had switched the plates. He returned the tool and stashed the removed license plate in the garbage

189

can. He looked up to find Gary Wraithworth in the doorway.

"Borrowed it, huh?"

"Give me a break, will ya?" Dennis said and raised his hand. "Got the thumb drive ready?"

"Workin' on it. About that... you're taking us with you."

"You two need to stay out of sight," Dennis protested. He stepped forward and Gary retreated into the house to allow Archen inside, where he found Tera sitting in the living room. "Hampton will kill you both."

"We can't just stew here, Dennis," she said.

"Not while you're out there, risking your life for us," Gary finished for her.

Archen ran his hand through his thinning hair, disrupting the tight curls at the back and sending them askew. "You two take the cake, you know that?"

The Wraithworths just smiled.

"You're good people," Dennis added. "Okay. Fine. Have it your way, but do me a favor," he said to Gary.

"What?"

"Get rid of that damned shirt," he told him and poked Gary on the *Wraithworks* icon.

"That thing's screaming your name everywhere we go."

Gary smiled. "I don't have anything else."

"In the master bedroom, you'll find some shirts that should come close to fitting."

Gary nodded and strode to the stairs. Dennis looked to Tera, who remained on the couch.

"I sure hope you two know what the hell you're doing," he said.

Chapter Fourteen

Gary and Tera got into the back of the SUV and stayed low like Archen told them.

It was a warm, partly sunny day, so Dennis put his sunglasses on and his short-brimmed fedora low on his head. He loaded his heavy black case in the back and they were away.

Archen and the Wraithworths had decided to head for the nearby Hennepin County Library, located in Hopkins, choosing time over safety. Dennis drove the SUV conservatively, obeying the traffic laws to the letter while his passengers kept their eyes open for a white Ford with a dented door. They saw a few similar vehicles on the short drive, but none were Hampton.

Dennis parked and the three of them shuffled quickly but casually into the library. Archen led the way to the information desk, where a pair of young women were paying attention to their respective computer screens. The older of the two, no more than twenty-five, looked up at the three people coming her way.

"Hello. Can I help you find anything?" she asked sweetly.

"Hi there," Archen began and removed his sunglasses. "Could you direct us to your computer section, please? My friends and I have to google some stuff." He smiled widely.

"Certainly," she answered then described the area and pointed off to her left.

Dennis thanked her, and the trio left the desk.

They were relieved to see most of the computers were available. Dennis gestured for Gary to sit at one and begin, which he did. Gary slipped the thumb drive from his pants' pocket and found the port at the front of the desktop unit. He opened the web browser, created a new YouTube channel, then began the video's upload. Once done, he uploaded it to his FylShareNet account.

He opened his email, found Daisy Hersh's address, composed an email, then attached the links to both sources. He did the same for their other YouTuber friends, Rup Williams, Trish Talbotz, and a slew of others they knew on a more casual basis, asking them to share the video and spread the word.

Lastly, Gary looked over his inbox. "Holy shit," he murmured, prompting Tera to lean over his shoulder for a look.

"Oh, my God," she whispered and clapped Gary on the shoulder. They smiled at each other.

"What?" Archen asked. From his seat next to Wraithworth, he could not see the monitor clearly. "What is it?" he repeated, allowing the infectious grins of his new friends spread to his face.

***

Anderson sat back in his office chair as he drank coffee and watched the television mounted to the wall above his four computer monitors, which were laid out in a half-octagon in front of him. It was another pointless news program on one of his employer's networks. The hosts were talking over and berating a guest joining them from another studio, set in split-screen and trying to state her case. Ken smiled. There was *no* point to any of it as the outcome might as well have been engraved in stone. Another one of his employers owned the power company whose shady business practices were the subject of the phony debate.

Public outcry was strong, but it mattered not a bit. The news about it would soon be suppressed and the masses would forget it and go back to their reruns and sports programs.

A light ding from the monitor at his far left interrupted his amusement. He looked over at it and noted the little box in the corner. It was his chatbox, kept open and dedicated to some of his many monitoring programs. This one was currently watching the Wraithworths' email addresses and had been a source of annoyance for several days. The Wraithworths were a popular couple.

The flashing red dot at the bottom of the text message grabbed Anderson's attention. This meant a login had happened. He grabbed the remote and muted the television as he turned his chair to the computer.

He clicked on the message to acknowledge it and switched to his spy tool's tab. There, he found the live feed of Gary Wraithworth's email account. As he watched, email after email was opened, skimmed over, and left as the user moved on to the next one.

Kenny Anderson cussed loudly in shock when he read the email address of the next one that opened. It featured the letters 'd' and 'g', followed by a series of numbers. As he read the email, he reached for the cellphone on his desk and initiated a call.

"Yeah, you're not going to like this shit at all," he spoke into the phone.

* * *

Del had just put his stolen Nissan in line at the fast food joint's drive-thru when his cellphone buzzed.

"Ken," he acknowledged and listened to the familiar voice. Anderson rarely got excited and almost never raised his voice, but the speed at which the man spoke concerned Hampton. "Okay, so what is it?"

"David Greely. He's not dead."

"Get the hell outta here!" Del nearly shouted. The vision of the burning Chevy played again in his mind's eye. *How in the world did the man escape that inferno?*

"That's what it looks like. I'm monitoring Gary Wraithworth's email. One is from an address Greely was using for the *RydingtheRails* channel."

"Read it to me," Del ordered as he guided the Nissan out of line and into a parking space.

"'Guys, all is well with me, though I'm hiding out until all is over. I forgot to tell you about a friend of mine. He is coming to see you sometime soon. I don't want to give you his name here, in case my emails are hacked, but my friend is short with dark hair and will tell you who the Killer Agent is and how he knows me. Take care.'

"No signature, but that has to be Greely."

"Track the IP," Hampton directed.

"Already on it, but it's taking the computer a long time. That usually means a re-router's been used."

"Stay on it," Del insisted, fuming behind the wheel. His stomach growled, his swollen wrist throbbed, and the lack of sleep was wearing him down. "Where is Wraithworth accessing from?"

Kenny launched the email hacking program's tracking feature. Here, it would trace the IP address to the source. "Just a minute."

"Any word from the locals about that SUV?" he asked to pass the time.

Anderson glanced at the computer monitor behind him, where he was keeping track of Eden Prairie Police's dispatch system. "Nothing yet." He turned forward once again. "Ah, okay. Wraithworth is accessing the internet from Hopkins, Minnesota. That's just north of Eden Prairie. Looks like the county library."

Hampton threw the Altima in reverse and pulled out in front of another car. The driver slammed on the brakes to keep from hitting the Nissan and laid on the horn. Ignoring it, Del headed for the exit.

"Give me the address."

***

It had been Archen's idea to forward the video to newspapers and television stations. He explained that there was more than enough national attention with the death of Charlie Durand and the discovery that David Greely still lived, to keep the momentum going. The Wraithworths were minor local celebrities, which held a certain degree of credibility, he had told them, and Gary and Tera agreed. While Gary searched the internet for the contact information of local news channels, both radio and television, Tera used another computer to spread the video to her friends and newspapers.

Dennis paced silently and watched the streets beyond the library windows. It was well past noon and they had all been in the library for almost an hour. He wished he had not suggested contacting the media from there. Having Del Hampton in the area was dangerous enough, but the Wraithworths' internet activity was like baiting the shark.

Gary cursed aloud, earning a frown from a nearby librarian, a woman in her sixties.

"What?" Dennis asked and stopped his pacing to look at the monitor.

"I got interrupted on that last email," Gary explained as he re-typed his password. Suddenly, it was invalid.

"Shit…same here," Tera said, this time earning a loud 'shush' from the librarian. "Sorry," she whispered.

"Okay, you guys," Dennis said and gestured frantically for them to follow him. "Time to get outta here. They're onto ya."

Without a word between them, Gary and Tera closed their sessions and quickly followed Archen, aware of the suspicious glances they were gathering from patrons and library employees alike.

Dennis placed his shades on his nose and took a peek through the front doors before allowing the Wraithworths to go outside. There was no sign of a white Crown Vic or any other police vehicles around, so he went through the door.

"Come on," he urged, in a jog. "We gotta get you two back to the house," he called over his shoulder.

Gary was glad he had changed out of his *Wraithworks* t-shirt and into the burnt orange souvenir that screamed the greatness of the State of Florida, though it may not have made any difference in the library. To the security cameras, he had no protection. He had left his sunglasses at home and wore no hat. His face would be quite clear. Tera was not as well-known, but by association, there would be no disputing who she was.

Gary tugged Tera along by the elbow as they tried to keep up with the much shorter Archen. The three of them boarded the big black SUV without a word.

"Let's get the hell outta here," Dennis said as he started the motor. Just as he reached for the gear shift, however, his eyes focused on a car that had just pulled into the parking lot and blocked their way. "Aw, come on, guy!"

"What is it?" Gary said from the back seat.

"Just some moron," Dennis answered.

It was then that the window of the Altima slid down, and a familiar face was revealed, his lips stretched into an evil grin that appeared to bend from one ear to the other. Then the barrel of the big handgun appeared just before it spat fire and lead.

The rounds struck the grillwork as Dennis dropped the shifter into reverse. Tera screamed, as did Gary.

"Get down and hang on!" Archen shouted. He need not have said so, as the big SUV accelerated backward, leaving Gary and Tera to slide off the leather surface of the seats and onto the floor. The rear tires shrieked, and the motor howled as more gunshots sounded and the rounds drilled their way into the metal. Dennis pushed the truck hard, steering left, then right onto the street.

"Was it him?" Gary called over the engine noise.

"Yeah," Dennis answered through a grimace. He watched the road ahead and his mirrors but steered with his right hand.

"Holy shit! Are we hit?"

"Yeah," he said and nodded. "It's the radiator. We're overheatin'!"

***

Del saw the panic on the driver's face as he drew recognition. The parking curb in front of the truck was no guarantee the sneaky driver could not bound over it and hit him, so he acted quickly, firing a few rounds into the engine block. His fifth shot pierced the windshield. As the SUV reversed, he hesitated, debating whether to take a shot at the driver or the tires. The SUV driver decided it for him by steering the truck toward the exit, where Del had entered. He fired two shots into the door as the black truck accelerated past him.

Hampton howled with laughter, even though the gunfire just inside the vehicle made his earplug-stuffed ears ring anyway. He threw the Altima in reverse and bounced into the street from which he entered, then gave chase. He cursed the underpowered four-cylinder of the Nissan and wished he had kept his Ford. After a few blocks, there was little gain on the truck, though as he watched, white smoke erupted from the truck's engine compartment.

"I've got you, son-of-a-bitch!" he shouted. Nearing a red light, he slammed on the brakes and steered around a stopped cab.

Two cars had screeched to a halt when the smoking SUV drove through, so Del stomped on the gas pedal. He ejected the 1911's empty magazine, slapped the next one into place, and replaced the gun to his shoulder holster. He put both hands back on the wheel and concentrated on catching the damaged SUV.

***

White smoke obscured Dennis's view of the road. The cabin was filled with the sweet scent of coolant. The needle of the temperature gauge was rising quickly.

He knew he had to do something drastic to lose their pursuer.

He let off the accelerator pedal, allowing Del Hampton to catch up. As he pressed the brake to stop for the next light, he watched the Nissan grow larger in the mirrors. The light changed to green, and the oncoming traffic would keep Hampton from pulling alongside. The cars ahead would take a few seconds to get going.

"What's going on, Dennis?" Gary shouted from the back seat. He and Tera had just pried themselves from the floor.

"Just stay down back there," he told them. He put the transmission into neutral and, with great effort, moved his left foot onto the brake and put the gas pedal halfway down with the right. The soon-to-be-destroyed eight-cylinder roared in their ears.

Dennis saw the Altima brake hard and swerve right, then left. Just as Dennis thought, Del was trying to see if he could get alongside or ahead of the SUV. There was nowhere to go, however, so Del came to a stop just behind the SUV.

"Hang on!" Dennis shouted and popped the gearshift into reverse. The entire drivetrain shuddered violently just a heartbeat before the rear tires cried out.

The Wraithworths had buckled their seatbelts and grunted against the strain as the truck shot backward. A second later, an impact pressed them hard into the seats. Both Tera and Gary squeezed their eyes closed.

Glass shattered, metal crunched, and plastic crumbled. The rear-end of the SUV hopped into the air and, for a moment, everyone inside thought it would tip over onto the driver's side. Instead, it rocked like a ship on a stormy sea. Then, it roared forward again, leaving tire smoke and debris behind.

***

Del pushed the Nissan for all it had and, considering it was only a four-cylinder, it was not falling behind the SUV too badly. He was able to keep it within sight, with the help of some traffic. After a short time, the traffic lights went against his quarry, trapping them behind several cars.

As he flew up on their rear, he steered the car to the left, crossing over into oncoming lanes, only to find that oncoming cars would keep him from getting next to the SUV. He jerked the wheel back to the right and slammed on the brakes. As the stolen ride came to a stop, he noticed the reverse lights of the truck come on and the distance between them shrank fast.

"Oh, shit!" Del shouted and tensed his entire body. The truck's rear end quickly filled the windshield and hit the Nissan hard, detonating the airbags. Hampton's vision went white then dark. He had the sensation of moving in reverse, well after his body had collided with the airbag and his chest compressed painfully against the seatbelt.

A second later, the sedan struck something at the rear, pressing his body into the seat, which broke and reclined.

Hampton was left dazed and when he opened his eyes, he found himself looking at the off-white headliner. At first, he did not know what it was until his eyes found the dome light. He blinked a few times to focus and got up on one elbow.

All he could see through the space that once held the windshield was the Altima's destroyed hood. Glass was everywhere, and when he moved, tiny pieces fell from him and clinked together like diamonds in a cloth pouch.

"Hey! Are you okay in there?" a young man's voice called through the now windowless driver's door.

"Maybe," Del croaked.

After a short struggle, the man freed the jammed door. Del sat up and accepted the helping hand. He grunted in pain as he stood.

"Are you all right?" the redheaded stranger repeated. He looked Del up and down.

"You've got a couple cuts on your face. Can you move everything?"

"Yeah, I think so," he said and reached into his inner pocket. He retrieved a handkerchief but revealed his shoulder holster in the process.

"Whoa!" the young man said and raised his hands as he took a couple steps back.

"It's okay," Del said and patted the bleeding cuts. "FBI."

A crowd was gathering around the site, and Del saw that the black SUV had managed a getaway.

A short blast from a siren announced the arrival of the first police cruiser. The officers hopped out and approached.

Hampton produced his badge and showed it to them. "I need some help, gentlemen."

***

It seemed like a minute had gone by before Gary realized that Dennis was shouting something. He shook his head to clear it and looked to Tera, who was slouched on the seat, holding onto the door armrest with both hands.

"What?" Gary called to their driver.

The air passed through the cabin in a loud whoosh and it was clear that, at the very least, the rear window was gone. The ride seemed extra bouncy and something metal was being dragged along the pavement.

"I said get ready to bail!"

Considering the ride so far, neither Gary nor Tera argued. Gary pulled himself up and looked about. The SUV was in shambles, with the interior trim work and fabric pulled from its mountings. The rear end was askew and vibrated as the truck labored along.

Wraithworth deduced what had happened and laughed giddily. "You rammed him!"

"Betcher ass!" Dennis confirmed. "I think he's out of the chase. I need to stop. When I do, get out!"

Gary looked again to Tera, who was badly shaken. She sat up and mouthed the words, "I'm okay."

As the truck was guided into a tight left-hand turn, the engine gave a loud bang and went silent. Dennis slipped the transmission into neutral and coasted to a stop.

"All right! Get out!" Archen shouted at them and opened his door.

Tera did as she was told but stopped short once she realized where they were. Gary nearly plowed into her as he followed.

"This is the hospital," she said. Her eyes went wide, and she gasped as she watched Archen slide out of the ruined truck.

Gary took a quick look over his surrounds and recognized the emergency entrance of Park Nicollet Methodist Hospital. He turned to Dennis and found the man struggling to stand. Blood ran from his lower left leg.

"Dennis!" he shouted and went to the man's side.

"I'm all right, just go!"

Tera said not a word as she sprinted for the emergency room entrance.

Gary put his shoulder under Archen's left arm and grabbed him around the waist. Together, they hobbled toward the door.

To take his eyes from the horrifying scene of the bleeding leg, Gary glanced over his shoulder at the SUV. Certainly, it was totaled. It still oozed white smoke from the grill and the entire body looked twisted.

"Sorry about your truck, Dennis," he offered, not knowing what else to say.

"It's okay. It was stolen."

"*What?!*" Gary squealed and halted.

"Kidding. I'm kidding," Dennis said with a crooked grin. Nearly out of breath from fighting the pain, he said, "Come on, get me in there."

Gary continued forward, letting their new friend lean on him. "Not funny. So not funny."

Tera burst through the automatic doors, followed by two nurses steering a gurney.

Dennis handed Gary a set of keys and his cellphone. "Here. Get back to the house. Grab a cab or somethin'."

"Are you sure?"

"Yes, I'm sure," Archen insisted and winced in pain. "Pull the battery outta the phone or the GPS will lead 'em to ya. Save it for an emergency, destroy it after. Get the box…back of the truck. The blue folder… take it with you. It has a copy of the report on Hampton."

"Blue folder. Got it."

"Okay, you two get goin'," Dennis hissed to Gary.

Wraithworth nodded and handed Archen over to the two nurses, who assailed them all with questions. He said nothing as he took Tera by the elbow and stood by the ruined SUV. One of the nurses directed the couple to follow inside to fill out some forms, but Gary had no intention of doing so. Police would be called in, and they still had no idea where they stood with the law. Tera got the gist of Gary's hold on her arm and relaxed.

Once the nurses had control of the gurney, however, Gary and Tera slipped out of their sight, standing behind the smoking truck until they had taken Dennis inside.

Gary climbed onto what used to be a bumper and reached for Archen's black box. It was scuffed and cracked, but its latch opened easily. Removing the blue folder, he hopped out. Gary went to the passenger side rear door, yanked it open, and fished out Tera's purse, his camera bag, and his laptop. He shut the door and looked around. They had gathered some curious glances from passersby.

"Come on," he said quietly to Tera and pointed across the two-lane road. He broke into a jog and she followed.

Beyond a vast row of fences, they could see the peaks of roofs. Seeing what he planned to do, Tera protested. "Gary! I can't climb that!"

"Sure you can," he insisted as he shoved his laptop into his camera bag. It barely fit into the largest pocket and there would be no way to zip it closed. The sound of sirens came to them from only a few blocks away. "Look, we have to get out of sight," he said and pointed to Archen's smoking truck. "The fire department's coming for that and the nurses have most likely already called security and the police."

He bent down and clasped his hands together. "I'll boost ya. Get going!"

Tera let slip a whimper of trepidation, then planted her right foot into his hands. As she propelled herself forward, Gary lifted. With a girlish squeal, she grabbed onto the top of the cedar fence and threw a leg over. From there, the other followed. She held onto the top of the fence for a moment, then realized her dangling feet were just inches from the grassy ground on the other side. She let go and stepped back.

Her husband's fingers were the first to be seen coming over the top, followed by his head and shoulders. He pulled himself over and dropped to the ground next to her.

As the sirens became louder, the Wraithworths took off across the backyard of a stranger's house.

Chapter Fifteen

*T*he email was received and opened by an employee of KSMP-TV's Editor of Submissions. Finding it of interest, she forwarded it to her boss. The editor, upon reading it and watching the video, forwarded it to the station's executive director, Christina Lohmiller.

It was Monday, and the rare solar eclipse was turning out to be a major disappointment with the sporadic cloud cover. She clicked on the link to the video sharing site and watched.

The host referenced the murders of Thomas Mackelby, the Pennsylvanian politician and Maxwell Jackson, the Democratic hopeful for the Ohio governorship in the last election.

She was not familiar with Gary Wraithworth or his YouTube channel, but by the time he mentioned the death of Charles Durand from Louisiana, and that the YouTuber from St. Louis that was thought to have been killed in a car fire was actually alive, she was on the phone with KSMP's producer, telling him simply, "Get in here."

Her producer watched the video and quickly informed the research department to verify the facts.

Within a half hour of the first viewing of Wraithworth's new video, it was found that the FBI and local law enforcement were actively searching for the couple. That they were considered armed and dangerous did not sit well with Lohmiller. Based on the video, neither Gary nor Tera seemed to be the criminal type.

While the notion that David Greely was not dead could not be verified, her researchers had uncovered videos from YouTube and some less popular sites, which featured the Killer Agent in action.

Together, the upper management of KSMP saw it all. The fact that the Wraithworths were a local couple made this big news.

After ordering writers to work up the story, Lohmiller grabbed her cellphone and texted Janine Tabor, her manager of field reporting. The lunar eclipse had made it an 'all hands on deck' sort of day, so all crews were already out on the streets.

"We have a hometown couple on the run from FBI and local police. Check your email, see the vid I just forwarded. Get it to the attention of all mobile units."

***

Still a bit hazy, Hampton stood about the scene, trying to collect his thoughts.

A crowd had gathered around and a few people, more than one of them police officers, had engaged him. Four more Hopkins Police cruisers had arrived, as did a paramedic unit. One of them cleaned the blood from his face and applied a disinfecting spray and a couple of bandages to the cuts. Del politely refused to be taken to the hospital for further examination, using his ongoing investigation as an excuse. He was left alone after that.

Hampton casually looked over the damage to the car. There was no way to get into the trunk to retrieve his bag. The car's rear end was compressed by the collision into a minivan.

He moved to the other side of the Altima, pretending to be fascinated with the damage the car had taken.

The glass had shattered on both doors, and he could see that his laptop was destroyed. His aviators had been crumpled at the nosepiece, and lay lense-less in a cupholder on the twisted center console. His briefcase, on the passenger side floor, next to the damaged laptop, appeared unscathed.

He felt the breast of his suit jacket and found that his cellphone was still there, so he was still in business.

As he was about to reach in to retrieve the computer and briefcase, he gave a glance around. A white van, just parking at the curb near the first police car that had arrived, caught his eye. KSMP-TV News was painted in big blue and red lettering. The doors opened, and three people filed out quickly. One well-dressed female, certainly the talent of the trio, one male in a jean jacket, and another with a large camera on his shoulder stepped out.

"Shit," he whispered and pulled his case and laptop from the car. He stood and looked for the cop that had first come up to him. "Sergeant," he called and strode over to him. "Any update on that APB?"

"We have a vehicle matching the description you gave," the policeman answered and gave his mustached lip a brief scratching. "It caught fire at the entrance to the emergency room at Park Nicollet. The driver's been shot in the leg and is in their care. Yours?"

Elated that he had, at least, caused one of them injury, Hampton saw no reason to lie. "Yeah. Look, can someone get me over there? I'm on their trail and I don't want it getting cold."

The sergeant nodded and found a nearby officer. "Larrette," he called to her and she approached. Looking to the FBI man, he said, "Agent–?"

"Hampton," Del answered.

"Agent Hampton needs a ride to Nicollet Emergency."

"Yes, sir," she answered and nodded at Hampton. She turned to her cruiser, parked at the intersection to the east of them.

Del got into the car, laying his briefcase on his lap. They set off for the hospital with lights and siren running.

"So, what are these people wanted for?" Officer Larrette asked her passenger. She had become instantly uncomfortable with the man, and even more so now that he was in her cruiser. The man's predatorial presence filled her with dread. He smelled of cheap men's aftershave lotion and sweat. She drove a little faster, anxious to get him out of her car. In the corner of her eye, she saw him slide the broken computer into the briefcase. The tilt of his head in her direction told her he was keeping her in his peripheral vision.

"It's a grocery list of things," Del conjured.

Larrette drove skillfully through traffic, her eyes darting every direction at intersections. At one pass to her right, she saw that Agent Hampton was still looking at her. She had expected him to continue speaking, but he went silent. She was glad that the hospital was not far.

She had been a policewoman for many years and had tangled with a lot of tough, nasty people, both men and women, but her spine tingled with the feeling of helplessness, despite being armed with a nine-millimeter pistol, a Taser, and pepper spray.

Normally, she would put some creepy man who stared at her in his place, but she felt this one was different. The image of a coiled snake came to mind.

Just beyond the next intersection, the sign for the hospital came up. She was never so glad to see it in her life.

***

Dennis Archen lay uncomfortably in the emergency room bed, having had his bleeding stopped and the wound bandaged. They had given him morphine at a low dose, which had taken the edge of the painful gunshot. He had just drifted to an intermittent, noise-addled sleep, when a man in a suit entered the glass-partitioned cube.

"Mr. Archen?" the man said and pulled his suit jacket open so that Dennis could see a badge at his belt and a gun at his side.

"That's me." *Here's where the shit hits the fan*, he thought.

"Detective Svenson, Hopkins P.D.," the tall, light-skinned man said. He had short blond hair that had turned gray at the temples. He had probably been clean-shaven that morning. He stepped inside the cramped area, followed by another, younger man, similarly dressed. "This is Detective Melrose."

They paused for a moment, sizing him up, so it seemed to Dennis. He nodded and mumbled a greeting.

"We're here to find out just what the hell happened in the streets of my beloved town," Svenson said more sternly, fixing his gray-blue eyes on Archen's face. "We've got reports of a car chase. Confirmed by witnesses. Exchanged gunfire, also confirmed by witnesses at our library."

"Nuh-uh! There was no exchange, I was the sole recipient of said gunfire," Dennis protested. A flash of anger surged through Dennis and he forced himself to sit up. "I don't have a gun. It's all that crazy asshole, Del Hampton. He's a rogue fed."

Svenson glanced at his younger partner, rolled his eyes, and smiled.

"Just look at my truck! Look at the car *he* was in. He shot at us, so I backed into it to get him off our asses. There's not a bullet hole in his car. I swear to God!"

"We'd love to have a look at your truck, Mr. Archen," Melrose said. "I'm afraid it's burned up pretty good."

"There'll still be holes in it!"

"And just who are the Wraithworths anyway?" Svenson followed.

"With any luck, it'll show up on the news tonight and you'll see," Dennis proclaimed. The pain in his leg flared but the morphine kept him weak and lightheaded. He settled back into the mattress and closed his eyes for a moment.

"Just who are you, Mr. Archen? Do you have any ID?" Svenson pressed.

"I'm a licensed private investigator," Dennis answered and pointed to the clear plastic bag his belongings had been transferred to once his pants were removed. "ID and business cards are in there."

Melrose stepped past his partner and picked up the bag. Rummaging briefly through it, he found the wallet, then the credentials. He showed them to Svenson.

"So, Mr. Archen, you do realize that the license plate on your SUV was stolen," Svenson said.

"Yeah, I know. But look, it was necessary. You don't understand."

"I understand you're wanted by the FBI, as are the Wraithworths."

"It's more than that, Detective," Archen said and adjusted the bed forward. "The FBI agent we were running from… he's not legit. I mean, he is an agent, but he's a dirty agent."

Melrose and Svenson looked at each other and sighed nearly in unison.

"Why don't you try filling us in then? From the top, Mr. Archen," bid Svenson.

***

Gary had the cabbie pass the entrance to the driveway of Archen's friends' home. He paid the fare and gave a tip that would not receive any memorable attention by being either too little or too large.

Tera followed her husband closely, keeping her eyes searching for anything unusual or sudden movement. As much as the thick grove of trees was comforting, there was plenty of cover for anyone that may be lying in wait.

Gary strode up to the front door and began to match the key with the locks. It took only a moment. The locks were high quality, and the strangely-shaped key was obvious. They walked inside, and Gary locked the door behind him.

Tera immediately turned on the television and scanned through the local channels.

Gary sat on the couch and removed his laptop from his camera bag, setting it up on the oversized coffee table. He left Archen's blue folder inside.

"Damn," he blurted and sat back hard.

"What?"

"The wi-fi is password protected," he explained. After a moment's deliberation, he pulled Archen's cellphone from his pocket, attached the battery, and powered it up. He searched through Archen's email app, scanning further and further back in time. There were a few emails regarding the investigations into Del Hampton, and not all of them were conversations with David Greely.

Searching further back, he found an email from a few days earlier with 'Crash Palace' as the subject line. As he searched through the email chain, he found that the home he and Tera were hiding out in was owned by Mr. and Mrs. Theodore Gerstner. He and Dennis discussed times and flights, how the fridge would be stocked, and that the key would be kept in the usual place. Lastly, Dennis had inquired about the wi-fi password and Gerstner had replied with it.

"Ah-ha!" he shouted.

"What now?" Tera asked, sounding quite tired and a little irritable.

"I have it."

She gave a soft grunt of understanding and let her head drop back onto the comfortable couch. She turned her head in the direction of the television but let her eyes close. The primary story on everything, including the weather networks, was the coverage of the lunar eclipse, an event that had occurred overhead with little notice from them.

Gary connected the laptop to the home's wi-fi and jumped onto the internet, disguising the IP address by going through his usual overlay network. He checked his email, happily noting that his message to Daisy had been received.

Gary and Tera,

I hope you guys are okay. You both look pretty freaked out in the vid. My channel's still suspended, but I'm making a new one to share this and will be posting everywhere with whoever I can reach. We'll see what happens.

Daisy

Gary showed the email to Tera and she smiled. "Hey, are you thirsty?"

"Yeah," she answered sleepily. "Hungry, too."

"I'll get you something," he said, kissed her, and left the couch.

Gary went to the kitchen and located the lunchmeats, cheeses, and a couple of tomatoes. As he made sandwiches, he wondered how their rescuer was doing. Archen had risked his life for them.

Gary felt a pang in his chest, thinking of what pain Dennis could be going through. It was a certainty that the hospital had called the police when they received a gunshot victim. *What was Dennis telling them? Did he dare speak truthfully?*

He had finished building the sandwiches and was about to return everything to the refrigerator when Tera yelled his name.

<u>Chapter Sixteen</u>

Detectives Svenson and Melrose were seasoned enough to know they were about to hear a story that would take some time. Both men grabbed chairs and sat listening to the wounded private detective's story, occasionally sharing crooked grins of doubt, but mostly, they remained expressionless as they handwrote notes on their pads.

Svenson interrupted. "So, you're saying that you came out here to protect the Wraithworths. What prompted that move?"

"Simple," Archen declared. "David Greely was in more direct contact with Wraithworth than Daisy Hersh."

"Hersh is the one you said was more popular on YouTube. Why wouldn't this rogue agent, as you call him, target her first?"

"When Greely crashed his car, I *knew*…just knew that Hampton was responsible. Hampton was after both Hersh and the Wraithworths, but I knew he'd come here before heading to Denver for Hersh."

Svenson and Melrose glanced at one another again. The answer seemed to sit well with both men. Detective Melrose took a deep breath, ran his hand through his thick black hair, and flipped his notebook back a few pages.

"Let me go over this a little with you, Mr. Archen," Melrose said. "You're saying that this Agent Hampton is responsible for all these crimes, political assassinations, abductions and so on—"

"And the murders of Durand and Greely," Dennis inserted.

Melrose nodded. "Right. Then you drove here in time to find him abducting Gary and Tera Wraithworth. You followed him to the parking lot of the funeral home, where you crashed into Hampton's car door, pinning him in place while you got the Wraithworths out of the car."

"That's right."

"And then he shot at you on two occasions. Once at the funeral home as you drove away, and then again when he found you three at the library."

"Yes," Archen said with a hint of exasperation, nodding emphatically as he pointed to his wounded leg. "That time he got me."

"Then he chased you and you backed your SUV into his car and then came here," Melrose finished.

"You know it better than me," Dennis replied.

"And you say that you don't know where Gary and Tera are?" Svenson pressed. He had asked the question before, but this time his voice dripped with doubt.

Archen gazed at the older detective for a moment. "I told you. If The Council can plant a man like Hampton into the FBI, they can get close to your department. I can't tell you."

Svenson sighed. "We can protect them, Archen."

Dennis took a deep breath, held it for a moment, and let it out slowly. Svenson and Melrose both looked sincere, but he was sure they did not fully believe him.

***

Gary jogged back into the living room to his wife's side, seeing that her eyes were glued to the television. She had left it tuned to the local news, which had begun its four o'clock broadcast. He tapped her shoulder with a cold can of diet soda. Absently, she took it from him.

The female anchor was speaking, but Gary had not focused on her words. He was aghast to notice a picture of himself and Tera and, in a moment, realized that it had been taken from the video they had sent the station.

"Holy shit, they're fast!" he blurted, and Tera shushed him.

"*...an Eden Prairie couple are on the run from what they claim to be a rogue FBI agent. This agent is said to be the man featured in footage taken from security cameras over the past few years, and in videos that have surfaced on several YouTube channels, many of which have since been suspended. YouTubers are determined, however, to spread these images of the 'Killer Agent,' as he has been called, seen here in stills—*"

The anchorwoman was replaced by a short slideshow of Del Hampton's grainy images, all of which the Wraithworths had seen before in David's videos. In this condensed, fast-forward style, the story behind each of the crimes was no more telling of the story than a set of flashcards was to a child trying to learn math, but their story was getting out.

Tera let out a whoop and clapped her hands. Gary felt as if a great weight had been lifted from his back.

"*—is suspected of the abduction of author Bill Welks, and the murders of New Jersey journalist Faiza Atiyeh, Ohio candidate for governor, Maxwell Jackson, and Bloomsburg, Pennsylvania Mayor, Thomas Mackelby.*"

As the anchorwoman went on to describe the abduction from the Eden Prairie City Center parking lot and their eventual rescue by what she called, "an unnamed Good Samaritan," Tera grabbed her husband's hand. He saw that she was tearing up, a scene that always threatened to do the same to him.

Gary crouched next to her. "It's all right. We'll be all right. So will Dennis."

Tera nodded and wiped her tears from her face with her other hand. "Not completely. Not until this asshole's in jail. I just hope the cops can protect Dennis."

***

Svenson and Melrose turned to the sound of the curtain parting. A tall, gray-haired man with an expression of intense seriousness entered. The detectives noted the cuts on his face and the bits of snagged material of his suit jacket. Without having to ask, they knew it was the FBI agent in question before the man had even raised his badge.

Svenson shot a look over his shoulder at Archen, who had gone white and speechless. His reaction was all the confirmation he needed.

"Gentlemen," the tall man began, "I'm Special Agent Del Hampton and you have someone of interest. I'd like a moment to talk with him, please."

"Detective Arnold Svenson," the policeman introduced as he stood. "This is Detective Tom Melrose."

Hampton acknowledged them with a nod. "I'm after a married couple by the name—"

"Wraithworth. Yeah, we know."

"Ah. Good. So, this man admits to knowing them," Hampton said and pushed in between the policemen. His eyes settled on Archen and an evil grin, unseen by Svenson and Melrose, sent chills through the wounded man.

"You guys! Get this monster away from me!" Archen shouted in panic.

Ignoring it, Del turned to the young detective on his right. "Do we have ID on this man?"

"Yes," Melrose said with a hesitation. He glanced at Svenson, who shrugged. Melrose reached into his pocket and pulled Archen's business card, handing it to the agent.

"Hmm," Del grunted. "Dennis Archen, Private Dick. Great."

"Detective Svenson, please," Archen begged as he stretched to see around Hampton. "This is the guy that shot me!"

"As you absconded with two fugitives wanted by the FBI," Hampton continued for his victim. "You bet I did." He took his cellphone from his pocket and texted Kenny Anderson, giving him Archen's information from the business card.

Anderson responded immediately with, "*On it.*"

"This is the guy from the videos," Archen went on as his eyes shifted from Melrose to Svenson and back. "This is the Killer Agent from YouTube! The one that the Wraithworths and Greely were covering!"

To this, Del Hampton laughed and eyed the detectives with a conspiratorial smile. "Yeah, that's only part of the reason the Bureau is after them."

Svenson and Melrose smiled back at the agent, though a bit uncomfortably. Svenson opened his mouth to ask what other crimes the Wraithworths had committed when the agent went on.

"If I can have a few moments alone with him, gentlemen, I'd appreciate it."

"No! Don't go!" Archen yelled. "He'll kill me! Please!"

Del Hampton rolled his eyes at Svenson and smiled. "You guys have men outside, right?"

Arnold Svenson gave a curt nod.

"He's not going anywhere. I just need a minute to ask him a couple questions and I'll leave him in your custody," Del Hampton promised with a car salesman smile.

***

Svenson and Melrose agreed and, despite the protests of Archen, stepped outside the partition and slid it closed. When they did, they both saw Agent Hampton pull the curtain, not to close it, but to open it further. He gave the two Hopkins Police detectives a nod and gestured with his finger that it would be a minute.

"Wow," Melrose commented as Archen's voice could be heard in the hallway. "That guy's either legit-scared or that's a hell of a put-on."

Svenson said nothing, trying to make out the private investigator's words. He could not. Hampton had stepped to the other side of the injured man's bed. Stepping over to the window, he could see both men clearly.

"You think we should have let him in there with him, Arn?" Melrose asked.

Svenson shrugged. "We're right here. They'll be taking him into surgery in a few anyway. What could it hurt?"

Tom Melrose nodded as he gazed into the room where a tense conversation was commencing between the agent and their victim, who would most likely be prosecuted if what Hampton had said was true.

"Do you believe a word of it?" Svenson asked his partner. He could not decide for himself.

Melrose shrugged and slipped his hands in his pockets. "I think it's interesting that this Hampton guy has a pretty nasty bruise on his right wrist."

Svenson moved closer to the glass. "And Agent Hampton never even mentioned it," he said lowly to Melrose. "Wouldn't you have arrested Archen on the spot for vehicular assault?"

"Yup."

"Archen's statement that Hampton had shot at them at the funeral home confirms the report of gunshots from that area earlier today."

***

As soon as the detectives stepped out, Del grinned and slowly moved to the curtain and spread it open.

"Now then, Mr. Archen," he began and stepped around to the other side of the bed. He smiled when he saw just how frightened Dennis Archen had become. "I would love to torture the living piss out of you...just for fun."

"You crazy bastard, stay the hell away from me!"

Del shifted his eyes to the two detectives just beyond the glass. "Tell me how you came to be in a position to rescue Gary and Tera, Dennis. Are you guys old friends?"

Dennis Archen turned his head away, taking little solace from the fact that Svenson and Melrose were just outside. He heard a click near his right ear and his blood ran cold. The edge of a switchblade touched his neck.

"Tell me how you're involved with this and where the Wraithworths are," he demanded. He glanced to the window and saw that Svenson and Melrose had turned away. He balled his fist and punched Archen's upper left leg. Though it was not the side where the bullet had entered, he knew that the round itself was in there somewhere. The loud grunt of pain told him that he was right.

***

The synthesized sound of a tiny bell ringing came to Kenny's left ear as he searched YouTube for channels showing Wraithworth's latest video, which was springing up like dandelions in a meadow. As soon as he removed the it from one channel, it would appear in three others. Everyone who had a channel, from the urban explorers and ghost hunters, to the conspiracy theorists, ufologists, backyard mechanics, and gourmet cooks were sharing the video, or even recorded themselves watching it 'live' and giving their reactions.

Anderson glanced to his left and saw that a new communication had come across the instant messenger. It was a note from his spy bot. A mobile source had accessed the email address he had found connected with Dennis Archen, Private Investigator. Not only that, but the GPS in the cellphone was still active.

"Yes!" he exclaimed and turned to the machine. Bringing up the inbox, he found the email to Mr. Theodore Gerstner. It was a simple matter to match up the Gerstner address with the GPS location. They matched.

Kenny yanked the phone's receiver from the cradle and tapped a saved number. "Sir, I have the likely location of the Wraithworths." He waited for the reply. "Hampton is interviewing the private investigator that liberated them earlier this afternoon," he explained and listened to the instructions that followed. "Yes, sir. They are on their way. I'll update their instructions," he said. He ended that call and made another.

**

234

Hampton knew he had little time before the detectives or a nurse would poke their heads in, especially after Archen's last yelp of pain. He folded the knife, replaced it to his pocket, and took a half-step back from the side of the bed.

"You know, Archen," he said through gritted teeth, "I don't give a shit whether you tell me where they are right now or not." He leaned into the private investigator's face and met his eyes. From that close, Hampton's were nearly black and completely heartless, like a shark's eyes just before they rolled back and the mouth opened to feed. "We'll find them, and as soon as I get a chance, I'm going to hunt you down and fucking bleed you."

"I'm not stupid, Hampton," Dennis replied, trying to halt his body's trembling. "I know I'm a dead man. I'm not telling you where they are, so just go ahead and kill me if you want. Right here!"

Del laughed and straightened up. "I'm not stupid, either, little man. Your time will come. Soon," he finished with a toothy grin.

"That's fine, Hampton," Dennis said, feeling a trace of the bravery he had felt when he pinned the agent with his truck. "I don't expect to live forever. I just want you to know that the days of The Council are numbered. Once the story gets out that your Nazi friends are manipulating the politics of the nation… and you're their hired assassin, it'll all be over."

Hampton laughed once more, though his eyes lit with a different emotion. He stepped closely to Archen and began patting him. "Where is it?" he asked then picked the clear plastic bag of clothes that had been set on the nightstand.

"Where's what?"

"Your recording device," Del said. "Where is it?"

"I don't—"

"Bullshit," Hampton cut him off. "That was an old-fashioned ploy, Archen. Right out of a late night detective movie."

"It's out of your hands, Hampton. Over!"

Del smirked. "Why don't you cut the shit and tell me where the Wraithworths are?"

Archen, figuring he had indeed played a poor hand, set his head back in the pillow. At that moment, Hampton's cellphone chirped.

"Yeah?" Hampton answered. "Ha! Really. Great, thanks." He tapped the screen to end the call and dumped the phone back into his jacket pocket.

"Well, it seems I don't need to ask you any further questions, Mr. Archen."

"What's happened?"

Del sauntered to Archen's left side with his hands in his pockets. Dennis shrunk away, fearing that the sociopath intended to strike his wound again.

"Your friends aren't as smart as they fucking think they are, you little shit," Del oozed and bent closer. He slipped his left hand from his pocket and dug the thumb into Archen's bandaged wound.

Dennis howled and pressed his palms against his tormentor but could not get him to move away. Instead, Hampton pressed his thumb into the wound harder. Archen screamed.

Svenson, responding to the sounds of agony, shoved the thick curtain out of his way and grabbed the FBI agent by the shoulders. Instead of moving, Hampton's right elbow came around, smacking the detective in the cheekbone and dislodging him. Svenson tumbled back, grasping the right side of his face. His vision had gone dark from the strike.

"Hey! That's enough!" Melrose bellowed. He rushed in and, grabbing Hampton by the outstretched elbow pulled the much larger man from the ailing Archen.

Hampton spun around and shoved the detective away from him, sending him tumbling into Svenson.

"Catch you, later, Archen," Del said over his shoulder. "Thank you for your cooperation, gentlemen." With that, he left.

Tom Melrose started after the agent, but Svenson took him by the shoulder. "Never mind that prick," he said and pointed to Archen. "Get some help in here. That wound's bleeding again. We'll post a complaint with the Bureau later."

Fuming, Melrose nodded and went out, calling out to a nurse for help.

Chapter Seventeen

Gary sat on the deeply cushioned recliner in the living room, physically comfortable but feeling out of place in the mansion. He wondered about their house, hoping that Hampton had not destroyed anything. He felt certain that the police had at least checked it out during their search for them. In his mind, he envisioned a team of men, covered in black body armor and carrying assault weapons, kicking in their front door and tearing the place apart as they searched for their fugitives.

Are we fugitives? Even with what's happened?

He turned his attention to his camera bag, reached inside, and pulled out Archen's blue folder, the one Dennis claimed had so much evidence. He opened it and perused the typed pages inside. It was quickly obvious that it was a giant report, if not an entire book, on the escapades of Del Hampton and The Council. The crimes went as far back as the early 1980s, with The Council recruiting Del Hampton straight out of the Green Berets. His entire military record was included, as well as his first few years with the Bureau. After that, he was considered undercover and his cases secret.

The members of The Council were documented by short biographies and photographs. Some were taken for the public, either for periodicals or company portraits. Others had the appearance of being candid, showing the members meeting with known white supremacists. Captions gave the identities of everyone in the pictures.

Coinciding with Hampton's dis-appearance from Bureau records, the first victims of unexplained murders were included in detail. Gary had never heard their names before, but as he skimmed the material, the sheer volume made his heart sink. This Council of billionaires, involved with everything from newspapers to steel mills, had attempted to control the flow of information and the political arena since 1982.

Gary paged through further, and as he continued, he found cases he was familiar with, written about in greater detail and highlighted with photographs. Toward the end, the cases were newer, and the pictures featured were taken from the videos Greely had shown them.

Wraithworth flipped through the pages more quickly, and at the end, found a list of contributors to the report. Just as Archen had told them, many were listed as retired policemen, private investigators, and some intrepid conspiracy-theorists-turned-YouTubers. It was a well-written report, highly detailed, and backed by credible witnesses.

"Holy shit," he said as he closed the folder.

"What?" Tera asked from the couch. The news had switched back to the story about the disappointing cloud clover that had ruined much of the lunar eclipse.

Gary told Tera of the contents of the blue folder and she gave him a weak smile.

"Well, that's something, then," she said. "We just have to make sure it gets to the right people."

He agreed and sat back in the recliner, letting his eyes rest. Before another thought could form in his mind, he drifted to sleep.

Exhausted, Tera soon followed his example and rested her head on the arm of the couch.

***

Hampton walked from the emergency room and gave a smile to the female officer that had driven him to the hospital. He had already forgotten her name. She gave a reluctant smile, but quickly looked away, returning to her conversation with two male officers standing with her. One of them eyed him with what may have been suspicion alone, but he detected a hint of contempt. Del dismissed it without a care.

Del exited the hospital and found that Archen's SUV had continued burning since his arrival, but the fire department had doused it. A flatbed tow truck was pulling in behind it. His feet splashed through the puddles of water as he stepped through the parking lot.

As Del typed the address Kenny had given him into his phone's map app, he kept an eye out for a new ride. With his laptop destroyed in the Nissan, his options were reduced to more direct methods. While he could easily have slipped inside one of the four Hopkins Police cruisers that bracketed the burned SUV, it would be found missing almost immediately and tracked.

His eyes soon found a young lady, dressed in maroon scrubs, walking with purpose in the next row. Her car keys were in her hand and a purse was slung over her shoulder. Her long amber hair fluttered behind her as she headed away from the hospital.

Del changed his direction and jogged toward her. For a moment, he thought she was going for a sandy-colored Mercury, but she passed it, stopping instead next to an old, roughly-treated Toyota hatchback from the last century.

It'll have to do, I guess, he thought and pulled the 1911 from beneath his jacket. "Excuse me. Miss?"

She turned to him and appeared delighted that such a handsome man was speaking to her. Her beautiful, white-toothed smile flickered and vanished when she saw the gun.

***

Sometime later, the sound of a sitcom's laugh track awakened Tera.

"Gare," she called from the couch, just feet away. "Gare!" she tried again.

"Huh?" he said and blinked the sleep away.

"What do you think we should do now?"

Gary sighed and looked past her to the window. The weak light coming through the tops of the drapes told him that late afternoon had turned into evening.

Out of habit, he began to look for his phone, but remembered that Del Hampton had destroyed it along with Tera's and he had not taken the time to put on a watch that morning. His thoughts led him to a dreadful discovery.

"Shit!" he shouted and leaped from the chair, searching the coffee table.

"What? Gary? What?!" Tera watched him, terrified he had heard something.

He found what he was looking for and snatched it up from the table. Cussing again, he showed it to her.

"So?" she asked, though in a moment, the problem became crystal clear. "Oh, shit, Gare!"

Even though he had remembered to close the web browser on his laptop, he had left Dennis Archen's cellular phone on, its email app open.

"Damn it," he hissed and pried the back cover from the device. He pulled the battery and let it all clatter to the table.

It was nearly seven p.m., and he realized they had been napping for more than three hours. He shut off the television and went to the couch. Putting his knee on it, he peeled the drapes back to look outside. The clouds were covering the falling sun, making the world outside gloomy.

"Gary, it's probably fine."

"Has anything been fine, today, Tera?" he nearly shouted. He let the drapes fall back in place and stood.

"Take it easy," she growled. "Maybe no one was looking for Dennis's phone's whatever…ID…serial number?"

"Hampton's got the FBI behind him," Gary reminded her. "Do you really think they aren't looking at everything?"

Tera stood up from the couch and stretched, though she remained silent. The sound of tires crawling over gravel came to her ears, freezing her in place as her eyes went wide.

"We've got to go. Now," Gary whispered.

***

Two nurses and the doctor in charge of the emergency room worked quickly to stop Archen's bleeding.

Svenson came close to the pained private investigator's face.

"Archen, what happened? What did you say to him?"

"He's gonna kill them both," Dennis replied and let out a long grunt as pressure was reapplied to his wound.

"The Wraithworths," Arnold Svenson said. Archen nodded through gritted teeth. "Where are they, Archen?"

"Detectives, I need to get this man into surgery. Now!" the doctor interrupted as the nurses unlocked the bed's wheels.

"One sec," Svenson shot to the doctor and put his hand on Archen's shoulder. "Look, I believe you about this Hampton guy. He's clearly out of the FBI's control. You have to trust us."

Dennis blinked through the pain in his leg and gave a nod.

"We have to go," the doctor said urgently. The nurses began moving the bed to the open doorway.

Archen blurted the house number and repeated it as Svenson and Melrose followed. "Indian Hills Road. That's in Edina. The Gerstner place. That's where they are. Stop that maniac!"

"Got it!" Svenson shouted after the rolling bed as he wrote down the address. Archen was guided through a set of doors by the nurses and doctor.

"Let me call it in. Get some units rolling," Tom Melrose offered as he pulled his cellphone from his pocket.

Svenson handed him the notepad. "Come on! We're going, too."

***

Gary ran into the den next to the living room and went to the window, leaving the lights off. He ran smack into a heavy chair, setting his

246

right shin blazing with pain. He peered through the blinds and, in the cloud-filtered orange sunlight, could only make out the shape of a car. It was small. A hatchback, he was sure, from the angular tail-end.

"Is it him?" Tera hissed from the doorway.

"I don't know," he answered. "It's some old import. Maybe it's just a cleaning lady or something."

"This late?"

"Yeah," he said, unconvinced by his supposition. The car stopped on the front lawn instead of the driveway, as if the driver was searching for light in the windows. "I don't like this at all."

"Gare. Come on," Tera urged.

"Yeah," he murmured. He began to move from the window, but just then, the strange car stopped.

The driver's door opened, and a tall figure stepped out. In the dimming light, all he could tell was that the person was male and had a full head of light-colored hair.

Gary Wraithworth sprang from the window. "Out the back," he said to her as he headed out of the room.

Tera ran ahead of him, taking a right turn into the kitchen, then another at the door to the

247

utility room. Just fifteen feet from the back door, her worn-out tennis shoes slid along the tile until she came to a stop. She looked behind her. Gary was not there.

She bolted in the direction she had come and again, stopped short. Gary nearly collided with her as he came around the corner.

He lifted the camera bag to show her. "We can't leave this stuff. I threw everything in here."

The sound of someone trying to insert something in the front door's lock was heard. It was a soft, metal-on-metal grating.

"Shit," Tera squeaked. She grabbed her husband by the borrowed t-shirt and, together, they scrambled for the back door. In the near-dark, she fumbled with the door chain, grimacing as it knocked loudly against the door once she had it free.

Gary followed his wife through the door, not bothering to close it behind him. They ran over the well-trimmed lawn, where the land became a sharp, damp decline. Beyond that was Arrowhead Lake.

Tera began to slip along the grass. Gary reached out and grabbed her by the arm, slowing her.

He turned to look back at the Gerstner's place in time to see the lights over the deck and the back door come on, ridding the area of the orange gloom. Gary could see the silhouette of Hampton in the window of the utility room.

In his mind, Gary flipped a coin. Choosing to run to their right, he tugged his wife's sleeve once again and they were off, sprinting toward unfamiliar territory. Tera quickly passed him.

Porchlights broke up the gloom of sundown and shadows, and a low brick structure appeared between the trees ahead of them.

"Fence!" Gary called and to his relief, Tera had seen it. She flung herself on it and quickly crawled over. Gary was slower, still clinging to the instinct to be careful with his camera bag.

A gunshot from behind and the loud crack of the round striking the brick right in front of him cast these inhibitions away. He leaped to catch the top of the fence and pulled his legs over, barely registering the bag's hard slap against it.

He landed clumsily, rolling along the grass until he could get his feet under himself to bounce back up. Seeing his wife waiting just ahead in a crouch spurred him on.

"Go! Go!" he shouted.

They ran along the uneven ground and soon found themselves out of the glow of electric light. Only the fading sun remained. Gary knew that, in a matter of minutes, his eyes would not be able to discern the difference between his wife and a tree trunk.

Over the sound of the pounding of their feet against the ground, Gary heard something else. As he watched his wife virtually fly over the brick fence at the other end of the large backyard, he was sure he recognized the howls of not one, but a few V-8 engines.

Gary made the mistake of halting at the fence to look over his shoulder. The red and blue lights of at least three police cars flickered and flashed through the thick trees that enshrouded the upscale neighborhood.

Behind him, unseen, Del Hampton caught a glimpse of Wraithworth's orange t-shirt and fired his 1911 again.

**

Melrose pushed the Charger hard to keep up with the other units ahead. Together with three Edina Police cruisers, the two from Hopkins and their own unmarked passed through traffic and wound down Indian Hill Road. It was narrow and curvy, though well-lit.

Svenson was quiet as his partner drove. The older detective trusted the younger man's skills, though a pang of anxiety shot through him once the units ahead came to an abrupt halt. Melrose crushed the brake pedal with both feet and steered a hard left. As fortune would have it, they found themselves in the Gerstners' driveway.

Detective Svenson quickly composed himself and glanced at his partner, arching an eyebrow.

Melrose shrugged and gave an embarrassed, boyish smile. "We're here."

The sound of a nearby gunshot stirred both men out of the car. Svenson noticed an old Toyota hatchback parked on the grass. It matched the description of the one carjacked from Park Nicollet. The nurse that owned it had been found unconscious on the hospital's front lawn. As they approached, Svenson saw the driver's door had been left wide open. A uniformed Edina officer jogged up to the detectives in a slight crouch.

"That shot didn't come from inside," he told them, pointing eastward.

Svenson thought a moment and pointed at the street they had just driven on. "This road runs around the lake, right?"

"Yeah," the officer answered.

"I think Hampton's chasing them. Get a couple units on the other side," Svenson ordered and ran toward the garage. Melrose was on his heels as two cruisers roared up the road.

Once around the garage, the two detectives moved quickly but cautiously eastward. Their guns were drawn but kept low as they searched for movement.

"Where the hell's that helo?" Svenson grumbled and cast his eyes to the darkening sky.

"Should be along any minute," Melrose replied.

The second gunshot cracked through the air, close enough that Svenson caught the flash in the corner of his eye. Without waiting for his partner, he sprinted in that direction.

Melrose did his best to keep up with Svenson, a spry man eleven years his senior.

***

As Gary climbed the fence to follow Tera, another gunshot sounded from close by, setting his ears ringing. Something hit his camera bag hard, feeling as if a man Hampton's size had kicked him. It was not until his feet landed on the ground that he realized his right side was getting warm. After a few steps, he made the horrifying discovery that the bullet had passed through the bag.

At first, he thought it was just a nick, but after a few more steps, the pain flared. "Oh, shit," he grunted.

Ahead of him, Tera was wading through water up to her ribcage. She had found a narrow stream joining the lake with a large pond to their right. Ahead of them and atop a hill was another large house, and the police cruisers lit the tree line beyond it.

Being shot had a strange effect. He did not wish to tell Tera he had been hit, so he doubled his efforts to run. He launched himself into the water, which he found to be pleasantly cold on the wound and pushed his legs hard to keep moving. For a brief span, the bottom of the lake went away, forcing them to break into a swim.

Together, they emerged from the cool water, drenched. Any concern Gary had for his computer, camera, or Archen's report in the blue folder was gone.

Gary could hear footsteps behind them. "Run!" he shouted to Tera, whose face he could barely see in the dim light of sundown. Her eyes widened in fear and she grabbed his arm and tried to run up the embankment.

Despite the cool comfort of the water, the swim through its immense heaviness drained his energy. His feet went out from under him when he tried to run with Tera and, as she refused to let him go, she landed in the dirt next to him.

"Gare!" she shouted. Wondering why her husband had dropped, she regained her feet and panicked. She tried desperately to pull him up by the wrist. "Gary!" she screamed.

"My God, woman. Shut *up*," Del Hampton called to her from the other side of the stream.

"Tera, just run," Gary said weakly.

"What? What happened? Get up!" she shrieked and tried pulling him again.

"Oooow, stop," he begged weakly. Each breath had become painful and his body felt too heavy to move. Furthermore, there was the anguish of failure. To have gone to such lengths to escape the madman only to have him kill them both was, by far, the worst of it.

"How's that feel, Gare?" Hampton jeered. He heard the thumping rotors of a helicopter. Looking north, he saw its search light covering the ground in its path.

Fast-moving footsteps came up from behind him and ahead, officers from the other side were searching the area with flashlights and would soon come down over the ridge. He lifted his 1911, aiming for Tera's head. If he could not prolong their torture, Gary Wraithworth would at least see his wife die before him.

"Hold it, Hampton!" someone shouted from behind.

Del rolled his eyes, knowing that if he fired on the couple in front of witnesses, the cover-up would be very difficult.

"FBI!" he called over his shoulder.

"Yeah, no shit!" another voice shouted. "Drop the gun or we'll drop *you!*"

The flashlights from ahead found the Wraithworths first and then the agent, apparently ready to end them. The officers on the Wraithworth's side of the water covered him with their weapons as the spotlight from the police helicopter found the scene and washed them all in white light.

"Don't be stupid, Agent Hampton," the one he now recognized as Detective Svenson said. "Put down the gun and turn toward us."

"Help my husband!" Tera cried in terror. In her mind, there should have been nothing stopping the cops behind her from advancing and dragging him to safety.

Del deliberated, not so quick to dismiss the possibility of shooting the Wraithworths and dying in the process. He was a patriot, after all, and had been trained to be prepared to forfeit his life for his employers, whom he felt were true Americans.

Svenson and Melrose took turns warning him off again and, in the face of the two uniforms on the other side of the water, who seemed cool and steady behind their pistols, Del made his decision.

"Fine," he grumbled and set the 1911's safety. He lowered it and tossed it to the grass behind him. Raising his arms to the sky, he turned slowly and faced the Hopkins detectives. "After all this fucking time, I let a couple of Barney Fifes get me," he said and rolled his eyes.

Svenson heard the siren of an ambulance, making its way slowly around Indian Hill Road. "Get those medics down here, fast!"

One of the officers near the Wraithworths holstered his weapon and ran up the hill. The other went closer to Gary and Tera.

"Get the cuffs on this smartass," Svenson ordered his partner.

Melrose nodded and holstered his weapon. With Svenson setting his handgun's sights on Hampton's forehead, his partner affixed the handcuffs on the man's wrists.

"You guys are going to lose your badges over this," Hampton warned with a grin. "When my superiors find out you've gotten in the way of my investigation–"

"Oh, shut up," Melrose said.

Svenson relaxed only slightly once the agent was cuffed. "All right, let's get him up the hill," he directed Melrose. Turning his attention to the officer attending to Gary, he said, "How is he?"

"Not sure. The round fragmented. He's bleeding from a couple places," the officer replied.

This statement sent Tera into fresh tears, though she refused to fall to hysterics. Her husband appeared to be asleep and his skin was turning ice cold in her hands.

With the paramedics now descending toward the water, Svenson knew there was nothing else he could do. He followed his partner up the hill.

***

"Back us up out of the light," the passenger ordered his driver. He sighed heavily out of tiredness and annoyance. His flight had been long and so had his wait for his partner, the man behind the wheel whom he barely knew.

They had arrived on the scene just moments before several police cars roared past them and his young cohort was inexperienced enough to park their rental directly underneath the streetlamp.

The driver did what he was told without comment. Moments later, the two of them watched their employers' right-hand man being shoved into a police car.

Quietly, the passenger pulled his cellphone and made a call which was answered on the second ring.

"Yeah?" answered Kenny Anderson.

"Bad news," the passenger said without emotion.

Chapter Eighteen

Gary awakened to a brilliant whiteness. He blinked slowly, turning it crimson, but when he opened them again, the world was again spotlessly white. The dream that he had been having, that of submarine duty in the vast Atlantic Ocean of yesteryear, began to fade. Somehow, the sonar pings remained. He turned his head toward the sound, stiff at the neck, and found the true source. It was a heart monitor attached to an IV stand.

The discovery was far from disappointing. He pulled the thin blanket up to his neck, trying to rid himself of a chill.

He lifted his head and found that he was alone. The windows across from the bed had their blinds mostly closed, leaving the sunlight to streak along the walls and ceiling. Lying perfectly flat, Gary shifted, and a bolt of pain shot through his torso. He let out a short cry.

He found the call button wrapped around the bed's guard and pressed it. In a moment, a nurse entered the room. She was dark-haired with a brilliant smile.

"Hello," she greeted. "I see we're awake."

He smiled. *Yeah, no freakin' kidding.* "Just now, yes. What's happened?"

"You're in Park Nicollet Methodist Hospital, recovering from surgery," she said a little too pleasantly for Gary's mood. "You took a few fragments of a bullet in your lower right side. They weren't too deep, and the surgeon got them out for you, but you're gonna feel it for a while."

"I do. Thank you," Gary replied sardonically, though smiling.

"I'll let your wife and the officers on the door know you're awake," she added as she helped him adjust the bed so he could sit up.

"Is Tera okay?"

"She sure is."

"I'm being guarded?"

"Yes, Mr. Wraithworth."

"As a guest or a prisoner?"

To this, the nurse laughed. "A witness, I'm sure. All I know is what I've seen on the news, so I'll let them fill you in."

"Um…what day is it?"

"It's Tuesday. You haven't been out of it too long. Just overnight," she said and grinned. After promising to bring in a pitcher of water, she left, shutting the door behind her.

Gary rested his spinning head onto the thin hospital pillow. The realization that he had survived being shot, that his wife was alive and well, and that the nurse had seen a news story about him, filled him with joy and trepidation in equal measure. His mind spun with questions and, quite suddenly, he was fully awake, and he wanted nothing more than to get out of the uncomfortable bed and find Tera.

Instead, the door opened again and a man wearing a suit walked in. The image of Del Hampton flooded his mind for the first time since before he had been shot. A flash of anxiety went through his body and Gary found himself pushing his fists against the mattress to rise.

"Whoa, there," the man said and took a couple of steps slowly forward. "Take it easy, Mr. Wraithworth. I'm Detective Arnie Svenson. Hopkins Police. Everything's fine. If you were expecting Agent Hampton, you can relax."

"Oh, good," Gary answered with deep sarcasm. "Can I?"

"Yes," Svenson assured him. "Hampton is in our custody. Turns out that the FBI is distancing themselves from this guy. They're giving us some bullshit story that he was transferred from one department to the next. Always going into deep cover from case-to-case, unbeknownst to any supervisor we've spoken to so far. They're still looking into it."

"Where's my wife?"

"My partner is getting her and a friend of yours right now. They went to get breakfast."

"The nurse said she saw the story on the news. What story?"

"The whole thing has spilled," Svenson said with a crooked grin. "We had a look at the videos on YouTube, Mr. Archen's file, a little water-damaged, and a cellphone picture of Hampton at a crime scene—"

"Ha! Which one?" Gary interrupted.

Svenson nodded and held up his index finger for Wraithworth to slow down. "—which implicates him in the attempted murder of David Greely and goes a long way to add credibility to everything else."

"Great!"

"There's more good news," Svenson added. "Hampton made a phone call from the station after his booking, and his handler or whoever it was refused to answer. We checked the number he dialed, and it was unlisted. I called it and verified that it was disconnected."

"So, what does that mean? Now what?"

"Well, we let him call another number, and that had the same result," Svenson explained. "He thought about it awhile and started talking. Hampton confirmed that he's a lifelong member of the Klan, and he claims that most of the men he worked for have strong ties with them and other white supremacist groups."

"Just like Archen's report said," Gary interjected.

Arnold nodded. "Seems like they've been trying to steer the country's politics by killing off anyone that was against their agenda. It's gonna turn into a real shit-storm for some influential people if he's telling the truth."

"You don't believe that The Council exists?"

"I didn't, at first, when Archen told us about it," Svenson admitted. "I have to say, though, as sociopathic as Hampton is, he's convincing and much of what he says matches Archen's documents."

The door swung inward and Tera stepped inside, followed by a tall, familiar dark-skinned figure in a long black overcoat.

"Tera—David!" Gary shouted.

Tera strode to Gary's side quickly and they kissed hello. Greely approached from the other side and shook Gary's hand.

"I'm happy as hell to see you both, but—"

"I know, 'how'd I do it?' Right?" David said and laughed.

"Well, yeah!" Gary answered and winced. He had shifted again, and pain flared.

"Take it easy, hon," Tera advised. "The doctor said the wounds aren't deep, but the bullet fragmented in your camera bag, and you were hit with two of them. By the way, you need a new laptop."

"Fine," Gary said, then put two and two together. "Oh! That's just fine," he said, patted her hand, and smiled. He turned to Greely and said, "So, tell me what happened."

"My crappy-ass car went off the damn road is what happened," David said and they all laughed. "Lucky it was a gentle slope and there were a lot of branches and junk. It cushioned the crash, and I got the hell out when the damn thing caught fire."

"Wow. Lucky," Gary said.

"Yeah," David agreed and pulled his cellphone from his pocket. He paged through his stored pictures and held it out for the Wraithworths to see. "This is just before I had to get out of there. He was tryin' to have a look to make sure I was dead."

The picture was taken from a short distance away, and Hampton could be seen through a thick grove of trees. To the right and further down the gulley was the burning hulk of Greely's car.

"I had to duck right after that. He looked my way. He tried to get closer to the car, but the whole area went up fast. I got the hell outta there and laid low till morning. I didn't know for sure if he saw the car was empty or not, so I grabbed a bus and came out here. Turns out, here he was."

"We saw that on the news," Tera spoke up. "How's your mom?"

"She's all good now," David replied and put his phone away. "She's embarrassed about how she talked to you, Gary."

"She can forget it," he said, waving it off. "I completely understand."

"Keep that pic, if you would, Mr. Greely," said Svenson. "Any little bit of evidence–" he trailed.

"I will," said David.

"I'll let you guys talk," Svenson said as he moved to the door. "We'll get a statement from you later, Mr. Wraithworth."

Gary happily agreed. Svenson stepped out and the door closed silently behind him. Not a second passed when it reopened. In rolled Dennis Archen, wearing a giant smile as a nurse pushed him into the room.

"Archen!" Greely blurted and moved to the man, grasping his hand in greeting.

"Hey, David!" Archen replied. "Great to see you're all right. I wouldn't believe it until I saw it."

"I'm all good, man."

"I saw the fire. I'm glad you got out."

"Me too," David agreed.

Dennis thanked the nurse, who then left. He rolled himself close to Gary. "So, how do you like being shot?"

"I don't. You?" Gary answered with a crooked grin.

"I'll pass next time, I think," Archen answered with an arched eyebrow.

"Was it bad?"

"It was really close to an artery, so I'm told. The surgeon was surprised that the car wreck didn't shift the bullet."

"Sounds like it could have been much worse, Dennis," Tera said.

"I was lucky."

"We all were," Gary added.

"And we got the racist prick," David said. He lifted a triumphant fist and Archen bumped it with his own. Gary followed suit, as did Tera.

"Let's just hope it sticks," Gary said with doubt in his voice. "It would be nice if his confession brings down this Council, too."

"You don't think it will?" David Greely asked in a tone of surprise.

"Money talks, David," Wraithworth said. "You never know. The prosecution could go light because the industries represented by members of The Council could mean too much to our

266

economy. And they can always bribe their way out of it and throw some underling under the bus."

"You mean…all this could be for nothin'?" Greely wondered with anger touching his voice.

"No, no," Dennis added. "Hampton's done…and The Council is done doing things their way."

Gary and Tera shared a glance.

"They're *done*, you guys," Archen stressed."

"I hope so," Gary said, and he meant it. He looked up to David Greely, who obviously needed some reassurance. "Dennis is right. Hampton's done. This was not wasted effort, David."

"That's right," Tera emphasized. "This is a good thing, you guys."

"That report of yours has them pretty tight, Dennis," Gary added. "It'll be interesting to see them try to squeeze out of it."

David smiled, but the seed of doubt had been planted. Gary noted it and was sorry he had said anything.

For a time, the four of them shared stories of the journey they had taken, separately or together, to get where they were.

***

David Greely gave his full statement, start to finish, to Svenson and Melrose. He went home on a bus the next morning.

Dennis Archen returned home a few days later but would not return to his private investigations for a few weeks to heal.

Tera was driven home that Tuesday afternoon by the police to the residence she shared with her husband in Eden Prairie.

Despite the presence of Eden Prairie Police cruisers that night, Tera could not sleep. She did not know whether it was a matter of Gary not being with her, or the thoughts of an uncertain future that kept her mind spinning, but the bed was cold and uncomfortable. She read a little, played games on her computer a little, and watched television until the sun came up that Wednesday morning.

Gary's wounds were healing well, so the hospital called her to take him home the following Friday morning. In safety, perceived or real, they dared not ponder, they slept the day away together.

__Epilogue__

*T*era tapped the button on the camera and stepped back. Her husband sat with his eyes set upon the center of the lens. He was eager to get this video, above all the others he had planned, recorded and uploaded. She could see the old Gary, lighthearted and upbeat, leaning forward, and full of energy. It had been too long.

"Hello, *Wraithworks* fans. It's Monday, October sixteenth, and today, we're covering the shocking news regarding The Council scandals. If you haven't heard, Del Hampton, the former FBI agent that was apprehended by Hopkins Police this past August has been shot and killed during a prisoner transfer in Washington D.C. just this morning."

Gary sat back, took a deep breath and let it out slowly. He folded his hands in front of him and tapped them on his desk before continuing.

"I have to say, everyone, I do have mixed feelings about this killing. Now, news is still trickling in about the shooting. I'm hoping no one else was shot, but we have to wait for further updates.

"As for the trials of Edwin Halloway and Jeff Kerroll, the two fall guys for their respective families, they are still the only two of the seven that have admitted to The Council's existence. Edwin's grandfather, Nathan Halloway, the big boss of their worldwide soft drink and snack food conglomerate, denies any ties with neo-Nazis, the Klan, or any other white supremacist group, as does Jeff's father, the oil baron, Jeremy Kerroll.

"This is speculation here, everyone, but Del Hampton's last appearance in court saw his confessions to the murders of Mishka Bellacosta of Dallas and Ariele Trujido of Chicago. Both, he claimed, were paid prostitutes for other members of The Council. No one's been able to locate Tony Etchins, the man last seen with Trujido. Tony is the son of oil tycoon Henry Etchins, and it's assumed that Trujido was killed to protect the family."

Gary paused to lean forward read from the laptop monitor at his right.

"Del Hampton claimed that he could not be specific about who gave the orders for these murders, and that's believable, considering Edwin Halloway's role of liaison for the group. I guess it's up to him to spill the beans on that one.

"Was Del Hampton killed by that sniper on orders from The Council? It seems plausible. What bothers me, though, is that would mean The Council is still in business."

Tera crossed her arms over her chest and silently took a deep breath. The thought had occurred to her as well, but Gary was the first to vocalize it. It had taken a few weeks for them both to become comfortable in their own home since the Del Hampton incident, and now, that giant butterfly had returned to the pit of her stomach.

"While the authorities still hunt for the alleged employees of The Council that were named in the Blue Report, we have yet to have the complete member list divulged by those taken into custody. And now, with the assassination of Del Hampton, there's one less until someone else is indicted.

"I guess time will tell, everyone. All we can do is wait it out. D.C. police haven't found the sniper yet, but it's early in the case. When they find the shooter, maybe he'll have more information.

"Until then, *Wraithworks* fans, I'm Gary, and I'll catch you next time. We'll be featuring a brand-new story, a missing persons case. Check it out tomorrow. Bye for now."

Tera counted a few seconds before stopping the camera. "Nice," she said.

"Think so?"

"Yup," she replied and sauntered to the door. "Do you want lunch now or do you want to get started on the editing right away?"

"I'll eat later. Thanks, hon." He smiled at her as she went out.

He had begun downloading the new video to the laptop for editing when he decided to check his email. He deleted the usual garbage that had not been flagged by the spam filter, skimmed over the messages that could wait, and found one from a sender that gave him chills.

Gary's heart pounded heavily in his chest and he felt his pulse at his temple. He thought to delete it, wipe it from his sight, and work on trying to forget it had ever arrived. He knew that would never work. They would not stop. Deleting the email from Mishka Bellacosta's hacked account would just escalate things.

He took a deep breath and clicked on it.

You should have dropped it when you had a chance.

Gary Wraithworth sat back hard in his padded chair. He felt paralyzed for a long moment, re-reading the sentence over and over again and wondering what to do.

With effort, he snapped himself out of his zombie stare and picked up his landline phone to make a call.

"Dennis. It's Gary," he said.

"Hey. How you doin'?"

From his friend's tone, he could tell something was wrong. "I got an email today."

"Yeah. Me too," Archen confirmed. "And I have to tell you, I'm starting to agree with whoever sent it."

About the Author

Frederick H. Crook was born in Chicago in 1970 and currently lives in Villa Park, Illinois with his wife and their three dachshunds.

Frederick writes daily and is also a freelance editor and proofreader.

Other Titles

The Fortress of Albion
The Interceptor's Song
Lunar Troll
Adrift
Runt Pulse
Minuteman Merlin
Campanelli: The Ping Tom Affair
Campanelli: Sentinel
Campanelli: Siege of the Nighthunter
Comfort in a Man Named Jakc
Of Knight & Devil
The Summer of '47

Made in the USA
Columbia, SC
21 June 2018